Beowulf, Wulfgar and Their Friggin' Horny Gods

First Edition

Published by The Nazca Plains Corporation
Las Vegas, Nevada
2009

ISBN: 978-1-935509-13-4

Published by

The Nazca Plains Corporation ®
4640 Paradise Rd, Suite 141
Las Vegas NV 89109-8000

PUBLISHER'S NOTE
Beowulf, Wulfgar and Their Friggin' Horny Gods is a work of fiction created wholly by *Tim Desmondes'* imagination. All characters are fictional and any resemblance to any persons living or deceased is purely by accident. No portion of this book reflects any real person or events.

Cover Photos,
Vladislav Gansovsky. Andrey Kiselev. Petr Podzemny.

Art Director,
Blake Stephens

Dedication

I dedicate this volume to a language.

A language? Are you nuts? No one dedicates a book to a language.

I do. I love this language of ours, our beloved English.

Old English began as a German dialect of the Angles and Saxons, lusty tribes of barbarians who conquered Britain in he fifth century and re-named it England. Their sagas like Beowulf and Wulfgar are classics of Old English.

Middle English followed the Norman Conquest in the eleventh century. Chaucer's Canterbury Tales are classics of Middle English. But many other lusty tales in that language like those about Robin Hood continue to entertain us.

Finally, Modern English, which includes authors from Shakespeare down to modern classics like the novels of Eleanor Tremaine delight readers around the world even as you read these words.

So here's to you, English – Old, Middle and Modern.

Tim Desmondes

Beowulf, Wulfgar and Their Friggin' Horny Gods

First Edition

Tim Desmondes

Table of Contents

Beowulf the Brave

Wulfgar the Stalwart

Those Friggin' Horny Anglo-Saxon Gods

Introduction

The Roman legions protected the shores of their province of Britannia for four hundred years against the attempted invasions of the Angles, Saxons, Frisians, Danes and the other barbarian tribes from the Continent.

But when the legions were called back to protect Rome itself from the invasions of Goths, Visigoths and Vandals, the defense of Britannia was left to the Celtic Britons who had dwelt on the island back when Julius Cæsar conquered and colonized it.

The Angles and Saxons took advantage of the absence of Rome's legions, invaded and wrested control of the Island from the Skots and Welch (tribal groupings of the Celtic peoples) driving most of them to lands at the north and south of the Island.

The language, gods and sagas of the Anglo-Saxons accompanied the victors who established their new kingdom of Angle-Land (England).

The earliest of the sagas in the English language to be recorded was Beowulf the Brave. The bards and minstrels sang Beowulf's story throughout the kingdom. More sagas were composed by the bards during the five hundred year span of Anglo-Saxon rule. The last recorded saga in the language which we now call Old English was that of Wulfgar the Stalwart.

So settle back and enjoy the tales sung by the bards and minstrels in Old English, translated, for better or worse, into Modern English.

Tim Desmondes

The Saga of Beowulf the Brave

Chapter One.
THE MEAD-HALL

Scyld was a great Angle king who, though an orphan, rose to become supreme leader of his people by force of will, strength and wit.

He set out from Anglia with a mighty force of warriors and women from continental Europe to establish his own kingdom on the Great Isle across The Channel.

When his ships landed at the White Cliffs, Woden and the other gods of Anglia and Saxony smiled down in approval.

In the course of time, the Angle warriors defeated the Celtic tribes that infested the Great Isle of the Setting Sun. So eventually the entire Great Isle was ruled by one man, King Scyld.

Scyld's son, Beow, was as great a hero as his father before him.

When death came to Scyld, as it must to all men, Beow placed his father's body in a deathship laden with great treasure, and released the corpse to the mighty sea.

What was the deathship's destination? Not even the wisest man on earth has ever determined the answer to that fateful question.

Beow ruled his people wisely and well and begat the mighty warrior Healfdene.

Healfdene possessed the physique of a god and was hung like a stallion. He satisfied not only his five wives but bevies of female slaves as well.

Healfdene's strength and bravery were bolstered by his sexual consummations. So his people were charged with keeping their king ennobled by supplying him with unlimited quantities of female flesh thus to maintain him as the kind of leader they required as a ruler of Angle-Land.

Healfdene begat Hrothgar, who became king at the moment he dispatched his father to sea in a deathship laden with such treasure as had never been seen before.

Now Hrothgar was as great a leader as the Angles had been blessed with up to that time. The soldiers of his tribe, who had been his boyhood companions, were fearless, fierce, brutal and loyal beyond imagination.

The Angles, like their Saxon cousins, were, and are, great lovers of mead, beer and wine. And the joys of the meadhall are their great delight. Their gods, Woden, Thor, Tugh, and Loki and the voluptuous goddesses Frida, Freya, and the hard drinking Brynhildr and her wild sisters, like their Anglo-Saxon worshippers down on earth, all relished their pint at the Valhalla mead-house as well.

Yea, drinking, wenching and brawling was and is the great delight of the tribes and gods of both the Angles and the Saxons.

By virtue of the bloodthirsty forages of his magnificent warriors wherever they marauded, Hrothgar's treasures abounded. Mighty was he in war against his foes. And as a monument to the renowned exploits of his tribe, he determined to construct a meadhall. Not such a paltry meadhall as could be seen on the moors, in the valleys, and atop the hills of his realm where lesser people made their habitations.

No. Hrothgar's was to be the largest, most lavish, and most riotous of any meadhall ever before seen or even imagined. His vision was to have a meeting and drinking hall to which his brave soldiers and their wenches could gather in ornate splendor.

Hrothgar's mighty squadrons went forth to highland, lowland, tor and tideland to bring back the building materials, thralls, and treasure necessary to undertake the construction of the great hall.

And when it was constructed, Hrothgar bestowed it with the name "Heorot (Hart)."

The high walls of Heorot rang with the sounds of feasts, orgies and brawls as well as the sweet and lusty songs and sagas of the bards, relating the tales of gods, warriors and lovers brought to the Angle-Land shores from the black forests of Anglia.

Joy reigned within Heorot for many a day, many a week, and many a year. Until the interruption of that vile ogre from the *Shittenmere* (sewage-swamp) located in the wastelands of the wild moors – Grendel.

In those days many monsters inhabited the world. There were giants and dwarfs, dragons, werewolves and zombies, vampires and gridleys, and other such despicable creatures whose names were sung by bard and minstrel alike.

Of those creatures, none was more loathsome than the gridleys who then, as now, dwelt in the nasty *shittenhusen* (privies) and *shittenholen* (latrines) where human waste is deposited by our race.

An entire marsh of fecal matter occupied the wilds of Hrothgar's kingdom, and residing in that foul marshland dwelt the noisome Grendel and his equally fetid mother.

Of these two shall we presently hear.

Chapter Two.
ENTER GRENDEL

One fateful night, following a riotous beerfest in Heorot, the mighty Anglowarriors had drunk, brawled, laughed, raged, and thoroughly enjoyed themselves to the full.

Overcome by their drunken stupor, they were not aware of the disgusting stench that preceded an ogre who had broken through Heorot's portals.

The unwelcome visitor was Grendel. Of such great size was he that no creature on earth could surpass him. More than five Anglomen could be held in his fist. The tracks left by his feet created craters in the ground. His member was of such size that no skald has ever ventured to describe it. And when his organ arose into a phallus the result was nothing short of awesome. And his testicles? They were comparable to boulders.

The evil ogre, begrimed and hungry, made ravenous by smelling the blood of the Anglomen, grabbed thirty of them and departed for the moorland laughing and nibbling.

First, he swallowed the heads whole. Then, one by one, the limbs. The soft tasty torsos he munched, followed by dessert that good taste forbids describing.

At dawn, the hungover drowsy Anglowarriors struggled awake to discover the disappearance of their thirty comrades. The craters in the form of footprints leading to and from the meadhall, tainted with human blood and bones, bore testimony to the fate of their fellow warriors.

The sound of weeping, wailing and gnashing of teeth thundered and echoed off Heorot's walls. Hrothgar's lamentations blended in with the grieving sobs of his mighty warriors.

The following night, Grendel returned to enjoy another lavish feast that awaited him in the magnificent meadhall.

The canny remaining warriors sought nightly refuge elsewhere, welcomed back into the arms of their previously empty-armed sweethearts.

And the meadhall, formerly filled with drunken warriors, stayed empty and abandoned night after night.

The lusty warriors had to resign themselves to libidinous pursuits rather than drinking and brawling the nights away. What a man can be driven to by a bloodthirsty ogre!

For twelve long years the meadhall was forsaken at night. Those nights were filled with romance. And while it was true that the tribe increased in number as a result, Hrothgar worried that the valor instilled by brawling was being leeched by enervating lovemaking.

Throughout the Germanic world, bards, minstrels and skalds broadcast the woes of Hrothgar. None of his warriors, even the bravest of the brave, had been able to kill the ogre Grendel.

Then cruelest blow of all occurred when Grendel abandoned his *Shittenmere* and moved into Heorot, spending every night in the midst of the huts of those he picked off for his nightly repast.

The Angles had no plan with which to put an end to their plight.

But, behold! Across The Channel lay the land of Saxony. The Saxons were blood cousins of the Angles. They shared language, blood, gods and legends.

Hygelac, king of the Saxons, welcomed a renowned bard to entertain his people in his meadhall. And the bard sang the woeful tale of the Lamentations of Hrothgar.

Among the warriors who heard the lugubrious recital was the strongest, mightiest, and noblest hero of them all. One whose ancestor, Healfdene by name, was an Angle. As was not uncommon at the time, Healfdene had sojourned in Anglia for a spell and had fathered a son yclept Edgetheow there.

Edgetheow begat a son he named Beowulf, who inherited the magnificent member of his father and his grandfather.

This well-hung young warrior heard the mournful tale about Heorot and Grendel and he was greatly moved.

He was aware that the Angle king, Hrothgar, and he, himself, were both descendants of the well-hung Healfdene. At some level, then, they were blood-cousins.

With the approval and blessing of his liege lord, Hygelac, Beowulf assembled a contingent of fourteen willing warriors to go to the assistance of the beleaguered Anglomen.

He acquired a ship on which to cross The Channel and, with a brave assemblage of heroes, he set sail for the White Cliffs of the Great Isle.

The well-armored Saxon crew, bearing bright, shiny spears and swords, stood proudly facing their western destination, born by a favorable wind across the foaming, choppy waters.

The gods observed the voyage of the Saxon ship and nodded approval at Beowulf's military excursion.

From atop the cliffs, King Hrothgar's watchmen observed the approach of the shipful of armored, armed warriors. Word went to the Anglowarriors to stand alert, for there was no way to determine whether the approaching warriors were friend or foe.

As the Saxons landed and marched down the gangplank to the shore they were met by a contingent of Hrothgar's army.

The captain of the Anglowarriors stepped forward and brandished his gleaming spear.

Beowulf stepped forward, his spear pointing into the sands of the shore.

The Angloman thane addressed the Saxon leader.

"Declare who you are and why you have traversed The Channel in yonder steep-keeled vessel. I and my men are here to confront anyone hostile to the Angles.

"You brazenly have arrived at our shores without our permission.

"I perceive that you are a warrior, clad as a warrior and armed as a warrior. You are of stunning appearance and the men aligned behind you appear to be worthy whether allies or opponents.

"Explain to me your name and lineage and your purpose in landing on our shores."

Beowulf, reversing his spear's orientation so that its tip pointed towards the arch of the heavens responded:

"I am yclept Beowulf, son of Edgetheow the Saxon, and subject to Hygelac the noble king of Saxony.

"As to my lineage, I am descended from Healfdene, the Angle, as is your king, the noble Hrothgar.

"We have come with hearts bursting with friendship to visit your lord.

"We have heard tell that a vile evil presence wreaks violence and slaughter on our Angle cousins. I come to offer our condolences for those of your tribe who have suffered. And further to provide such advice and assistance as may benefit his highness and his people."

The thane replied:

"I perceive that you are friendly to our lord king. I will lead you to the good Hrothgar and will leave here on the shore a contingent to guard and protect your ship so long as you visit our island."

Beowulf and his band followed their Angle hosts to the awesome ornamented meadhall.

Chapter Three.
BEOWULF MEETS GERDA

Beowulf and his brave companions were greeted at Heorot's portal by Hrothgar's herald, Weoxstan by name. When apprised by the captain who had led the gallant band thither who and what the visiting warriors were, the herald welcomed them:

"I will inform the Lord of the Angles, the giver of rings, of your arrival," he informed the visitor.

Weoxstan hastened to his liege, now aged and gray bearded, who was seated with his counselors in the counsel chamber annex of Heorot.

And thus he addressed King Hrothgar.

"From across The Channel has come a Saxon, a warrior chief yclept Beowulf son of Edgetheow. He and his men seek audience with your majesty. His band appears battle-worthy and he who leads them is of magnificent appearance."

Hrothgar responded:

"I knew this Beowulf when he was a boy. His father, Edgetheow is a kinsman of mine.

"Bards and minstrels sing of his warlike valor. It is recited that he has the strength of thirty men in his grip.

"The Lords Woden and Thor have sent this hero to us to save us from the terror of Grendel. I shall give treasures, yea, treasures, rings and women, to this man and his followers.

"Go in haste and bring this hero and his band to us that we may welcome him in the name of the Angle people."

Hrothgar was left wondering whether Beowulf had inherited the genital gift-curse of Healfdene. If so, he would have need of a personal sweetheart and a backup of female sex-slaves.

Not all of Healfdene's descendants were endowed with the stallion-pizzle. Lamentably, Hrothgar himself was not as splendidly hung as his ancestor Healfdene.

Weoxstan hastened back to the portal to welcome Beowulf.

"My Lord, the Master of Battles, giver of rings and King of the Angles, bids me tell you that he knows of your shared ancestry. Yea, even that he knew you as a child. Be assured that you and your band are welcome."

He escorted the hearty band to the privy chamber.

When Beowulf and his men entered the counsel chamber, one look at the hero revealed to Hrothgar the answer to one of his questions. For a glance at Beowulf's codpiece told him that the hero was endowed at the loins with Healfdene's genital gigantism.

The king arose and embraced his visiting kinsman.

Privately, in his cousin's ear, he welcomed him and told him he would receive him officially in the meadhall itself.

For the good king meant the reception of the brave band to be held before as many of his people as possible. But, more important, he wanted the unmarried princesses and the female sex-slaves present so Beowulf could chose a sweetheart from among the princesses and he and his men could select their comfort-women from among the slaves.

For a man with the endowment of Healfdene would have mighty need of a lusty sex partner and backups to maintain his strength and bravery. And his men would also need meretricious relief and entertainment.

Hrothgar dispatched Weoxstan to inform his subjects that a gala assembly was immanent in the meadhall. And to make sure that the unwed royal princesses be accorded prominent seats.

It was understood that the only slaves to be admitted to the gala were to be the ones whose sole occupation was pleasure-giving.

As the subjects and slaves entered the meadhall the king was already sitting on his throne on the dais with his counselors at his side. A bard was strumming his harp to fit the mood of the occasion.

When the doors were closed and the king raised his scepter everyone but the slaves who were standing along the walls sat down.

The bard, Onegar by name, sang a short lay praising Beowulf the Saxon.

At the conclusion of the rendition, the door to the counsel chamber opened and Weoxstan entered preceding Beowulf and his band. Everyone in the hall except Hrothgar arose.

The visiting Saxons knelt before the king. Hrothgar bade them rise, stood, embraced Beowulf, welcomed his band, and gave a welcoming speech.

When the king re-ascended his throne, the Saxon band faced the assemblage.

The princesses were prominently standing in the front row of the hall. As Beowulf's eyes grazed over the bevy his eyes met the voluptuous mammary adornments that graced the chest of Princess Gerda. When his gaze rose to embrace her lovely facial features, the twitch in his codpiece spoke volumes.

Gerda was not only aware of the greeting emitted from the hero's groin. The moisture that enveloped her crotch and the emergence of her nipples informed her that true love had just entered her heart.

As the fourteen members of the brave Saxon band cast hungry looks over the sex-slaves lined up against the walls of the hall, their physical responses assured sensual feasts ahead as well.

Beowulf turned his back to the crowd to address the king. The audience (other than the slaves) sat again.

"O King," the hero addressed Hrothgar in stentorian tones.

"I, Beowulf, son of Edgetheow the Saxon and kinsman and warrior of Hygelac, King of Saxony, am renowned for deeds of might and bravery.

"In my native land across The Channel, bard and minstrel have informed us of the monster Grendel. They recite how this illustrious hall stands idle every night after the sun has set due to the monster's occupation of it.

"I felt a call to respond to the misery of our cousin tribe. I have returned many a time to my own land drenched in the blood of our enemies.

"I have suffered pain all night long after destroying a nest of five giants. I have ground up sea serpents whose remains float still above the waters of the deep.

"I came here, O Lord of the Angles, asking but a single favor. Do not refuse me and my band the opportunity of cleansing Heorot of its scourge. I have heard that Grendel uses no weapons in his depredations.

"Thus, to demonstrate the valor of the Angles and the Saxons, I will enter battle bearing neither sword nor shield. Nor will I wear armor or codpiece. Even as the evil ogre engages in battle bare-fisted and bare-arsed, even so will I challenge him. With my bare hands will I seize the enemy and fight him to the death.

"Should I lose the battle, I doubt not that Brynhildr and her Valkyries will fetch me to Valhalla's halls and the embrace of Woden and his fellow gods. And you, fair king, need not concern yourself with burial rites for my mortal body. For the monster will bear away this body dripping with blood and gore, munching and nibbling on my flesh and bones.

"But if I overcome the beast in this battle, I will send his vile soul to *Hel* (Hell) where it will suffer such indignities as human imagination cannot fathom. And I will nail his scrotum to yon eastern wall of Heorot as a trophy to the valor of the Anglo-Saxon race.

"Yes, the will of *Lord Wyrd* (Fate) cannot be foretold and no armor can withstand his dictates. So, if it has been preordained that Grendel shall overcome me, I pray you send this shirt of mail that I wear to my liege Hygelac. The armor came to me as a legacy from Hrethel and was forged by the mighty smith Wayland."

Hrothgar formally granted the Saxon hero leave to occupy Heorot that night and to engage in hand-to-hand combat with the vile monster who had bloodied the meadhall with Angloman gore.

As beer, wine and mead was served to the crowd, Onegar composed a lay on the spot celebrating Beowulf's valor.

During the recital, slaves were driven back to their quarters and Gerda took Beowulf by the hand and led him from the hall to the *leofhutte* (love-shack) where the lovers consummated their devotion to each other.

The *leofhutte* was not dissimilar from those that graced every Anglo-Saxon community on either side of The Channel. It was dedicated to Freya, the goddess of youth and sexual passion. Its altar was a spacious bed dedicated to lovemaking.

Gerda, to show her acceptance of the pact ratified by mutual observance back in the meadhall, initiated the ceremony by the removal of her robe.

The sight of the golden orbed breasts punctuated by shining pink-hued nipples caused a pressure to be expended on the hero's codpiece.

Gerda's pubis consisted of a lovely golden triangle that focused Beowulf's eyes on a moist, waiting cunt.

The strain on the codpiece was inexorable. Beowulf had to remove the garment, otherwise it would burst or cause him exquisite strangling pain.

He divested himself of the hampering garment and followed the action by removing all his armor.

The two lovers faced each other in splendid nakedness.

Gerda opened her arms and as Beowulf clasped her to him they virtually merged one into the other.

A single glance had informed Gerda that oral copulation, at least by her, was an impossibility. She was a virgin princess but the Angle youths had no concept of modesty instilled in them and she had seen the male member displayed in full innocence often enough. She knew she could accommodate any of their penises into her oral cavity.

But the gigantic equipment of her heroic lover could never, under any circumstance, be thusly accommodated.

The exchange of tongues held no such restriction. Nor could the explorations each made of the other's body be contained.

Beowulf extracted his tongue from his princess' mouth the better to explore the welcoming nipples that twinkled pinkly at him.

Gerda's soft manual caresses explored not only the awesome phallus of her hero, but supported a pair of testes that promised a plentiful supply of love nectar.

In due course, the altar-bed received the couple in its embrace.

Beowulf well knew he would receive no oral succor from his mate. Many a Saxon lass had bravely attempted the feat. Only to find failure at the attempt. But to brave Beowulf that was no misfortune. For he mightily favored basic sexual intercourse.

However, as a prelude to his favorite act, he enjoyed matching his ravishing tongue to his partner's pleasure garden, with final flourishes upon the boy-in-the-boat.

When the need of the couple compelled them to perform the act, Beowulf's mighty phallus entered Gerda's awaiting cunt, and he emptied a joyful spurt of his nectar into her womb.

The couple could well have spent many an hour in further lovemaking, but they knew they would be expected back in the meadhall to partake in the drink fest.

So, reluctantly, they donned their garb and returned to join the festivities.

As the happy couple rejoined the throng in the meadhall, a merry racket resounded off the walls. One would be hard put to encounter a sober Angloman.

Wealhtheow, Hrothgar's queen, was bearing the ceremonial golden wassail cup, filled to the brim with honeyed mead to her husband, the thronèd king.

Hrothgar toasted his Saxon guests and the crowd cheered boisterously. The regal queen proceeded from table to table, sharing the wassail with each reveler, young and old, so that each could drink to the health of Beowulf and his brave band.

When all had loudly toasted the Saxons, many-ringed Wealhtheow brought the wassail bowl to Beowulf. She extended the libation to him thanking Woden and Frida that they had granted her prayer to send a hero to bravely confront the ogre. And she added her thanks to Freya that a worthy lover had arrived to grant libidinal comfort to her lovely daughter Gerda.

Beowulf stood to receive the wassail. Everyone in the hall became silent to listen to the words of the hero.

"When I boarded my ship to cross The Channel with my warriors, I swore that I, on my own, would rid your tribe of its nemesis or die in Grendel's grasp. I now take my oath to noble Hrothgar and all of you, his valiant subjects, that I shall do so or never more appear in this meadhall."

The bold-bedecked queen was pleased by the pretty speech and ascended the dais to sit next to the king on her throne.

The drinking and carousing continued until Beowulf felt a stirring at the groin that compelled him to rise and take Gerda by the hand.

He knew that the coming night would tax his strength and courage to the brink. In order to prepare for the battle ahead, he needed to store up his resources. So, he led a willing Gerda to the *leofhutte*.

The instant they entered the hut, the couple disrobed. The performance was a demonstration of their enthusiasm for the upcoming bout. Beowulf's egregious erection and the moisture instantly gathered at Gerda's cunt would have made instant copulation quite attainable.

But Beowulf was in no rush to return to the meadhall to await the visit of the monster. The place would not be empty of the merrymakers until a great deal more mead, beer and wine had been consumed.

And his previous sojourn with the ivory-skinned, golden orbed princess had been constrained by a need to get the deed done in short order so he could get back to the hall in time for the awaiting welcoming ceremonies.

Beowulf was a great admirer of the female bosom. And Gerda's golden orbs, embellished by the pinkest of pink nipples had not received sufficient attention in his previous visit to the hut.

When the princess stood, the enormous globes hung out invitingly. Kneeling before her, Beowulf's lips encircled the rosy aureoles as his tongue teased the protruding nubs. His large hands were filled with her orbs, massaging them with an expertise he had developed early in his life over in Saxony. While her lover was thus engaged, Gerda's hands ran lovingly through his long curly blond locks, played love games with his earlobes, reached under his chin and gave gently tickles that caused his organ to keep joyous time with the tunes her fingers were playing.

Beowulf arose, lifted Gerda off her feet and laid her gently on the bed-altar.

Straddling her body at its mid-section, he took a breast in each hand, pressed the orbs together, and inserted his phallus within the décolleté.

As he gave her what the Anglo-Saxons referred to as a *tittefukken*, Gerda was able to lave the underside of his organ with her tongue as that shaft performed its upward and downward thrusts past her exquisite mouth.

Indeed, she orchestrated the thrusting motion by gentle squeezes on his balls that otherwise would have simply rested on her midriff.

Many a minstrel has sung a lay about the sex-fest engaged in by the Saxon hero and his lovely Angle princess. Suffice it to say that wherever concavity met convexity, erotic opportunity was made of the discovery.

As Beowulf lay down beside her, their lovemaking having satisfied each to satiety, Gerda wondered whether she would ever again know the satisfaction of that evening.

The probability of her lover surviving his encounter with the immensely strong, brutal, bloodthirsty ogre was doubtful.

For too many an Anglowarrior had died a gruesome death at the gory hands of the tribe's nemesis.

The princess kissed Beowulf on the lips.

He arose from the bed, leaned over and gave her a farewell kiss, and strode out of the hut naked to go meet his destiny in the meadhall.

Chapter Four.
GRENDEL'S RETURN

Stretched out on the floor of the great meadhall, Beowulf awaited the arrival of the bloodthirsty ogre.

He lay fully reposed without weapon, armor, or codpiece. His enemy would arrive buck-*ars* naked. Without a stitch or weapon would Beowulf confront the threat.

The first inkling of Grendel's approach from the moor tickled Beowulf's nostrils. For the foul emanation that reeked from the monster's loathsome body filled the air for miles around.

The next clue to Grendel's approach were the sounds of the tramping of his enormous bare feet on the surface of the earth.

A cross between a mammoth grunt and a coarse belch resounded as the giant flung open the unbolted door and spied the Saxon hero sprawled on the floor.

The entrance of the fiend filled the air of the hall with noxious fumes.

The mighty warrior watched his foe's approach. The fire in Grendel's eyes and his slathering maw caused not fear, but a surge of anger, strength and courage, to invade Beowulf's heart.

As the monster reached down to grab the mortal Saxon, the drool from his mouth became a gush as he prepared to eat the morsel head first, limbs next, followed by torso and terminating with genitals. A gruesome laugh burst out of the ravening mouth.

But before the gigantic hands could engage his prey, his opponent, the great warrior of the race of men, grabbed first. Lightening quick was Beowulf's reaction.

Grendel's laugh morphed into a gasp of rage and pain. For Beowulf had a firm grasp of the ogre's balls.

No creatures outside the monster world were hung with testicles of such magnitude. The tight grip of the human exerted pain commensurate with the size of the glands involved.

Grendel was alarmed. He had faced spears, swords, lances and halberds wielded by metal clad men time and time again. To such weapons he was immune. But to be seized by his balls? This was an affront to which he was not inured.

Fear assailed the stinking creature. It was an emotion previously unknown to him. His cries of fear and pain echoed within the meadhall and were heard for miles around.

Flee! That was the only thought that occupied the giant's mind. But the more he attempted to move away, the tighter the grip of his human opponent.

Beowulf proceeded to twist the sack containing the giant orbs. Once around. A screech of such pitch as to awaken folk across The Channel issued from deep within the tortured giant. He strove harder still to flee back to his *Shittenmere*. With one more twist and a powerful yank, the testes were severed from the giant's groin as he rushed out the door and into the freezing night.

The woeful cries, screams and bellows of the beast awoke every one of Hrothgar's subjects. Hrothgar feared he had lost his brave guest to the ravages of the ogre. Gerda lamented that her well-hung lover was being consumed by the enemy of the Angles.

The bravest of the tribe peeked out onto the meadow. And there they spied Grendel running, staggering, lurching towards the moors.

Some foolish warriors grabbed their weapons to pursue the disappearing fiend. In truth, each should have been well-aware by then that weapons were useless against the scourge of their kingdom.

The blood cascading from the fiend's crotch filled his plodding footprints with gore. And the heather was splashed a crimson red by the discharge from his wound. The dreadful monster made it to the edge of the *Shittenmere* into which he plunged headlong.

Every hut of the people of Hrothgar's kingdom emptied into the cold of the night. The sound of rejoicing filled the air as the folk descended upon the magnificent meadhall.

They entered to observe Beowulf nailing the enormous sackful of testes to the eastern wall of Heorot.

Onegar was first to arrive and strumming on his harp he sang of the victory of the noble Saxon over the ball-less ogre.

Hrothgar, Wealhtheow and Gerda arrived in time to see Beowulf, his hand clenched around a hammer that would do justice to Thor's great weapon, drive the last nail onto the trophy that graced the eastern wall.

On the morrow, people came from near and far to marvel at the blood-tinged footprints leading from the meadhall off into the moors.

They followed those prints to the edge of the noisome mere where they abruptly stopped. Steaming gore floated amongst the feces.

Those who followed the gruesome trail returned to the meadhall to drink and sing the praises of the savior of the Angles.

Onegar was inspired to sing lay after lay praising Beowulf's strength and bravery and extemporized on how the Saxon had emasculated the foe.

When he had justly praised Beowulf in song, the bard sang and recited the epic about Sigord's battle with Vanir the dragon. It was the favorite epic of both Angles and Saxons. The hero, Sigord, had re-forged the shards of his father, Sigmond's sword, Nodhung. With it, he had slain the dragon, freed great treasure, made love to Brynhildr, and been born to Valhalla.

At great festivals, Onegar always recited the splendid epic to the strains of his mellow harp.

By the time he came to the conclusion, there was not a sober person sitting at Heorot's tables.

Chapter Five.
THE ANGLES CELEBRATE

Hrothgar, as drunk as any person still awake in the meadhall, left his throne and stood before the great trophy hanging on the eastern wall.

"I give great thanks to Woden and Thor for this sight I behold. The noble Beowulf truly had our foe Grendel by the balls.

"Until yesterday, I doubted our land would ever be rid of the curse of the monster's ravages.

"Today our whole nation rejoices and joins me in thanking the gods of Valhalla for sending the mighty one to our shore.

"Now, Beowulf, listen. Know that I love you as a son. Finely wrought golden rings, torques and armbands I shall give you. But for such a lusty hero as you it is not enough to receive trinkets. I will have built for your exclusive use two huts. In one, you will live as a prince with Princess Gerda as your consort.

"The other is a *leofhutte* to be occupied by four sex-slaves who will be yours alone to enjoy. Each has a specialty to keep you amused while you allow Gerda to recover from your lusty attentions.

"But that is scarcely all that we Angles offer you, Beowulf. Tomorrow at sundown we will assemble here. Heorot shall be especially decorated for the occasion. We shall feast on boar and deer and address our mead horns again.

"For now, let us all return to our huts and to the arms of our loved ones and to the arms also of Eofor, the goddess of sleep."

Thus bid, Beowulf shortly found himself disporting in the arms of the voluptuous princess who was his love. And after vigorous engagement, the two fell asleep in each other's arms.

During the years Grendel occupied the meadhall, Heorot had deteriorated.

By order of the king, it was now restored to its previous luster by exertion of craftsmen and thralls.

At sundown, everyone assembled in the spacious hall.

Gold-embroidered tapestries hung on the walls with designs that delight the very soul of man. Wherever the fiend had damaged the hall, workmen had repaired and embellished the blemish.

The scent of roasted boar and game deer permeated the atmosphere. Thralls bearing flagons of mead, beer and wine attended the tables.

In this festive atmosphere Hrothgar bestowed on Beowulf a gilded battle-banner, a well-wrought breastplate and a horned-helmet with decorated bands that would resist the strongest sword.

When offered the wassail bowl, the hero drank deeply.

Eight splendid war-horses were brought into the hall as gifts for the hero. One was adorned with a saddle gold plated and studded with precious stones. It had been Hrothgar's own battle seat when he had led his warriors into the battle after battle.

And to each of Beowulf's companions who had accompanied him to the Great Isle the king gave golden rings, armbands and torques. And in addition each of the brave Saxons was given a sex-slave to own for as long as she gave him pleasure.

While the joyful crowd ate, drank and cheered, Onegar entertained them with the story of how the Angles came to rule the Island Nation.

His epic song told the history of how The Island had become Angle-land:

Long before the arrival of Angles or Saxons, the crafty Celtic Britons had wrested the Island from the Druidic people. The religion of the Celts, Wycca, superseded Druidism on the Isle.

The Romans then conquered the Britons and occupied the land for four hundred years. The Roman gods mixed with the religion of the Hanging Carpenter towards the end of the Occupation.

At length, Rome called back her legions, tempting Angles to take their place.

The invading Angles were welcomed by the British king Vortigern, to serve as warriors against his own foes.

Despite their service to the British king, an upstart Celtic warlord named Arthur and his evil wizard Myrddin attacked the noble Angle general Hengest. They treacherously massacred the brave Anglo-warriors and emasculated their leader Hengest before the eyes of the survivors.

In revenge, Hnæf, the general and warlord of the Angles led his men against the hated Britons and established the Great Isle as Angle-Land.

This historic tale always raised the patriotic spirit of the Anglomen and their women. And the drunker the listeners became, the greater was the patriotic fever raised by the tales Onegar sang and recited to his rejoicing audience.

Not a soul left Heorot with firm step.

All, including Beowulf, staggered home to their beds.

In the following days, Beowulf made joyful use of the *leofhutte* that had been erected for him. His consort, Gerda, though a willing and enthusiastic partner to his amorous capers, was pleased to take respite from her lover's unremitting romantic attentions.

Truth to tell, she needed time to heal from the abrasions he incurred on her garden of delights.

Beowulf could have employed all four of his sex slaves simultaneously were he disposed in that direction. But in no way was the hero perverted in that direction. So, like a fine Saxon gentleman, he entertained his harem girls one at a time in accordance with their unique erotic ploys.

He dignified his slaves by giving each one a number. And so he bestowed them with the names *An* (One), *Twa* (Two), *Thre* (Three), and *Feower* (Four).

The girls, who were previously nameless, were delighted now to have distinctive names to call themselves and to call each other.

When Beowulf entered his newly constructed, beautifully appointed *leofhutte* the four lovelies were lined up to greet him in a state of stunning deshabille.

Beowulf disrobed himself so his slaves could take in his own masculine pulchritude. With one breath the concubines sighed with pleasure as they took in the utter majesty of the equipment it would be their obligation and pleasure to work with. Never was warrior more pleasingly endowed to engage with his Anglo-Saxon playmates.

Over the next four to five hours, Beowulf checked out the individual specialties of his slaves. He was engaged with each one close to an hour at a time. And during each engagement, the three slaves who were not at the moment entertaining their lord and master were enthusiastic spectators of the libidinous feature playing out on the opulent bed that dominated the hut.

To begin the love-feast, An, whose mouth and oral cavity were of awesome dimension, demonstrated that she could envelope her master's glans penis with her lips and perform pneumatic activities that brought a new delight to the Saxon. Beowulf had experienced fellatio before, when he was young. And had, indeed, enjoyed it. But with the physiological hormonal changes consequent to puberty and adolescence, his inheritance from his Angle forbearer Healfdene made the practice impossible because of the enormity of his member. That is, until he was given the orally gifted An who not only had oral capacity but a set of lungs that enabled her to suck up pints of nectar over the period she was allowed to satisfy her master.

After a period of rest and recuperation for the hero. Twa took her position on the altar-bed.

Twa's mouth was of normal dimension. But not so her tongue. That lingual organ emerged from her lovely mouth like a gorgeous serpent.

Beowulf lay on the bed, twisting and turning his naked body to expose himself incrementally to the wanton slurps of Twa's skilled tongue. That tongue explored not only the trail from perineum to ear-canal, it explored anal, navel and oral indentations.

But the greatest delight Beowulf found in Twa's ministrations were the tracing of saliva trails over his massive scrotum.

Thre was a different kind of delight from the others. She had a small vestigial tail and skillfully played the role of a hunting bitch in heat. She wiggled her *ars* invitingly as Beowulf, also on all fours, scampered after her. She led him a merry chase. Each time he caught her and mounted her she bayed delightfully.

The engagement did not continue for as long a time as Twa's licking fest. It was amusing to the hero, yes. But a half-hour romp at this sort of thing proved sufficient.

Feower proved to be the most fulfilling of the girls from Beowulf's standpoint.

Her breasts were voluptuous and eminently suckable. Her dainty fingers played arabesques over every erogenous zone of his body. Her vagina fit around his phallus so snuggly one would think it had been tailored exclusively for his personal use only. But best of all, she was an adept at the art of pompoir. With Beowulf's ithyphallic member cozily ensconced within her cunt she contracted the muscles of the vagina so as to cause a sucking sensation which caused sensations in his balls as though a surge of nectar arose from those might orbs to gush into her uterus.

Holy Thor!

Beowulf had made love to many a woman in his time. But none had ever matched Feower for pure sensual delight.

In addition to the pleasure of his sex-slaves, he knew he would always enjoy his sexual encounters with his consort Gerda.

Yet not Gerda, nor any of the other sex-slaves could or would ever give him the satisfaction of Feower.

Beowulf had been well-rewarded by King Hrothgar.

Chapter Six
AN ENCOUNTER WITH GRENDEL'S MUM

Now that there was no longer fear and concern over Grendel's incursions, the great mead-hall, Heorot, was occupied nightly by Hrothgar's warriors. They cleared the floor of tables and benches, spread out their covers and pillows and settled in to peaceful sleep with their helmets, armor, spears and lances within reach. For there was not a moment, day or night, when the king's warriors were not prepared to respond to the alarm of war.

None knew where the next danger might spring from. On this occasion it was to come from Grendel's pained, enraged trek from Heorot to the moors, his balls left behind in the hands of the naked Saxon warrior.

Wailing, and cursing, the monster had arrived at the banks of the *Shittenmere*. There he had let out a mighty scream and plunged into the stinking depths.

He sank down to the bottom of the *mere* and into the arms of his loving mum.

Grendel's father had left the *Shittenmere* for Ultima Thule ages before. We do not know much about him other than, like his son, he was a Gridley and lived in nasty *shittenmeres* wherever he encountered them.

Not so Grendel's mum. The *Shittenmere* was not her natural habitat. While her Gridley consort was present, and while her Gridley son lived with her, she was content to live in the mucky mire.

But she had been born a sea-monster in The Channel, not far distant from the White Cliffs. She bore the name Sæwulf (Sea Wolf).

Sitting among the turds, she clasped her dying beloved son in her claws and shed copious tears. In that wrenching moment Sæwulf was possessed by one compelling emotion.

REVENGE.

She was well aware of where her mischievous boy had gone to play his pranks and pick up a tasty snack or two. Heorot, the humans' feasting hall provided him with games and game.

So she resolved to pay a surprise visit to Heorot herself.

Sæwulf crashed into the hall one evening, pleased to see that it was filled with tasty Anglowarriors. She saw her son's severed scrotum nailed to the wall.

Grabbing the severed remains of her son's body with one hand and a couple of warriors with the other, she trod screaming her ear-piercing scream, which she stifled by consuming one of the hapless Angles on her way back to her home among the noxious refuse.

Beowulf was not in the great hall when Sæwulf paid her visit. He was quite occupied with satisfying Gerda's need for servicing.

Beowulf had been so occupied in tending to his consort's needs that he was totally unaware of the clashes in the meadhall or the victory howls of the sea-serpent.

He was aroused in mid-stroke by the insistent demands Weoxstan the herald was shouting at his door.

Beowulf rapidly donned his codpiece and was at Hrothgar's side with all due haste.

"Ah, Beowulf," Hrothgar wailed. "Torment again besets my people. Heorot was visited last night by a mighty female sea-monster. It was well-known to our people that Grendel was the spawn of a Gridley and a sea-serpent. There can remain no doubt that our midnight visitor was none other than Grendel's mum.

"She snatched up two of my most valiant warriors, one my trusted general Æshere, the other the warrior Fandal. When seen leaving the meadhall she had already consumed Fandal and held Æschere still in her hand.

"She had then snatched her son's ball-sack from the eastern wall of Heorot, bearing it I know not where.

"It may be that she headed back to the *Shittenmere* where she lived with her son. And then, again, she may be heading for the sea now that her son is dead. If we wish to encounter her, I have no doubts that she will have left footprints enough to follow.

"Again, as once before, I have no warriors who can withstand the force of such a monster as this one who has sullied our hall.

"I am now old and feeble," the king continued. "But I cannot die in peace until this final scourge is erased from our Angle-Land.

"I will reward you as never was hero rewarded before if you will undertake the quest to find this she-fiend and rid us of her presence."

Beowulf addressed the ancient king:

"My advice, O king, is that we proceed immediately in pursuit of this new monster who has desecrated your realm. Let us summon the bravest warriors available and chase down this dæmon even unto the gates of *Hel*.

"She shall not escape our punishment. Allow me leave to arm myself and don my armor that there be as little delay as possible in chasing down our prey and ridding the world of her foul presence."

Hrothgar, with Beowulf at his side, led his marching battalion in tracking Sæwulf. She was not the sort to protect herself by hiding. She did not attempt to cover her tracks leading away from Heorot. Blood, bones, and spit comprised her spoor.

The she-fiend clearly invited pursuit, for she left Æshare's head intact on her path, staring in the direction she was taking.

That direction was not towards the moors and the *Shittenmere*. Her path was clearly eastward towards her previous home, her cave beneath the waters of The Channel, off the coast of the White Cliffs.

At length the contingent arrived atop the majestic cliffs. Blood stained the sands below. And tracks led straight into the turbulent waters.

Sporting in the waters of The Channel were writhing sea-drakes and water snakes, serpents and other water-monsters.

Beowulf let fly an arrow that pierced the scales of a sea-monster, wedging in its throat. The beast thrashed and squirmed.

Down onto the shore went Hrothgar and Beowulf's band. The stricken monster had made for shore where the warrior band dragged the carcass onto the sands and gazed with wonderment on the grisly remains.

Beowulf prepared himself to follow his foe right into the deep. He gave not one thought to the monsters frolicking on the surface. He knew his prey lurked well beneath the surging foam.

Nor did he give thought to the danger to his own life. A true hero cannot function if he considers his own mortality.

His strength and courage were close to their height. When he had been summoned by Weoxstan to learn of the sea-fiend's incursions into the meadhall he was in mid-thrust of his fifth frolic with his consort. The only way his stamina and bravery could possibly have been even more enhanced would have been if his companion at the time had been that mistress of pompoir, Feower.

Preparing for his immersion into The Channel, the hero donned his shirt of fine meshed mail. He placed on his head his horned-helmet which was richly decorated and invulnerable to halberd or spear.

Onela, who was Hrothgar's spokesman, stepped forward bearing a wonderfully wrought sword in his hands.

"O brave and valiant Saxon warrior," he exclaimed.

"I am of the race of Volsongs. My people merged with the race of Angles in past ages. And this sword has been passed down from father to son over the generations.

"Tradition has it that this is the fabled sword Nodhung. Whether such be fact or not, it has never failed to win victory for its bearer.

"I yield this sword, with whatever power it may possess, into your hands as you prepare for your upcoming battle.

"I have not the strength nor valor to descend to the depths of The Channel to confront the she-devil who has ravaged, and, yes devoured two of my most beloved companions.

"Nodhung is worthy of one with greater courage than I possess. So here, O Beowulf, I offer it to you as a worthy weapon fit for your task."

Beowulf accepted the ancient sword with thanks. He then turned to address the king:

"O Hrothgar, King of Angle-Land. I request you to keep in mind what we have discussed before, now that I am about to undertake this adventure on your behalf.

"If it should happen that my death ensues from this endeavor, you will assume the responsibility of acting as my father.

"Protect my warriors, my comrades, my friends, as though they were your own. Send the treasures you have bestowed upon me to Hygelac, king of the Saxons, that he may know of your gracious generosity to me.

"And give to Onela my sword, which has faithfully withstood many a battle on my behalf, while I have wielded his sword, the ancient, revered Nodhung, against the she-monster of the deep. And with that wondrous weapon I will prevail or give up my life in the trial."

The words had scarce left his lips as he waded resolutely into the turbulent waters.

Many hours passed before Beowulf came close to the bottom depths of The Channel.

Sæwulf was scarcely unaware of the approach of the hero. She had expected a confrontation from the creature who had emasculated her son, and who had thus murdered him.

She lurked among the swaying seaweed, keeping a steady eye on his approach.

As Beowulf came within her springing distance Sæwulf bounded out from her cover and snatched him into her horrid claws.

But she caused no harm to the hale body contained within the coat of mail that protected him.

The sea-wolf dragged him to the deepest depths of The Channel and bore him to the mouth of her lair.

Once there, swarms of sea-beasts attacked him with their tusks and assaulted him in an attempt to cut through his armor. Their skirmishes were to no avail.

When they wore themselves out with their vain attempts, Grendel's mum dragged her prey into the sea-cave that was her ancestral home.

In that cavern, he was free from the weight of water and the attacks of the sea-beasties.

And the darkness of the deep did not bother him since a bright fire blazed within the space.

And the great warrior could perceive for himself the form of the monster. She was a kind of sea hag, a she-wolf of the sea, a monster who was as comfortable on land as on sea, and ferocious in any venue.

He rushed at her brandishing the mighty battle-sword Nodhung. He brought the weapon down upon the head of his foe. To no avail. She was immune to iron, steel, or weaponry of any kind wielded by man against her scaly skin.

Beowulf realized that he would have to fight her nude as he had fought her son. As he removed his garb, Sæwulf stepped back and observed with interest.

When Beowulf removed the suit of mail, her eyes came close to emitting fire. She had not seen such musculature in any male creature since her mate, Thordstinke, had left her and the baby and headed north.

She had had opportunities aplenty to mate since being abandoned by Thordstinke. But no creature, monstrous or otherwise had excited her female senses. How strange that this lowly human being, her son's murderer, had ignited her fire.

When he removed his final garment, his codpiece, his magnificent cock was revealed for her delectation. Her remarkably lovely breasts caused tingling in his balls.

Desire flickered first in Beowulf's breast then burst into flamboyance. And Sæwulf was filed with a passion to mate with this creature and then devour him stem to stern.

Her nipples extended halfway across the cave in his direction and her cunt dripped its elixir to the floor of the cave, drenching her feet.

As he viewed the magnitude of her passion, Beowulf's testes went into overdrive, forcing his equipment into the most powerful erection he had ever experienced.

Loki, the god of fire and mischief, getting wind of the confrontation, could not remain aloof in Valhalla. He was present in the sea-cave. But he was invisible to man and beast.

Loki whispered advice into Beowulf's ear. Gratuitous advice it was, for the very souls of both Saxon and Sea-wolf were already imbued with the selfsame urge: *Mate and kill!*.

Beowulf and Sæwulf approached each other with outstretched arms.

Sæwulf was drooling with appetite for a post-coital feast of her approaching consort while her cunt dripped with anticipation of receiving the Saxon superorgan.

Beowulf's intense passion caused his hardon to throb with anticipation of the carnal climax to come while his bloodlust burned simultaneously in his veins.

Man and beast met in mad embrace.

The climax of their orgasmic encounter was so intense Hrothgar and his force up on shore felt it as an eruption from the sea.

Loki slipped Nodhung into Beowulf's fist as the hero withdrew following his ejaculation. Sæwulf continued to spasm as her orgasms kept multiplying.

The hero's bloodlust impelled him to run Nodhung, the mighty sword forged by Sigord himself, up through the quivering vagina of the she-monster, up past her womb, and directly into her heart.

Unlike her son, the sea-wolf died in an ecstasy of delight.

Chapter Seven
THE YOUNG HERO

Up on the shore, Hrothgar and his men concluded from the eruption in the waters and the blood that was floating to the surface that the *sæwulf* was victorious and that the corpse of the hero now languished in her lair.

At noon, they gave up all hope. The king and his warriors returned home. Beowulf's Saxon band trudged up to the top of the bluffs and stared seaward. They could not give up hope that their leader would return from the deep. But it was hope with scant belief.

Down below, in the sea-cave, Beowulf still had the sword Nodhung in his grip. Standing over the corpse of his erstwhile lover-foe, he sliced off one of her enormous, gorgeous breasts to take with him back to hang on the walls of Heorot.

His eyes marveled at what was happening to the weapon after that blade swipe. The blade was melting as does an icicle before a blazing flame. The blood of the monster woman was eating away the metal that was disintegrating before the hero's wondering eyes.

The sight did not surprise Loki in the least. The god knew the sword was created to withstand dragon's blood. But the life fluids of such a creature as Sæwulf were too much for it.

There was treasure aplenty hoarded in piles in the sea-serpent's cavern. Such booty held no appeal for the victor of the fray.

All that he wished to take back with him was Sæwulf's breast and the hilt of Sigord's sword.

He re-donned his horned-helmet, armor and codpiece, and, hilt and trophy in hand plunged back into the waters of The Channel.

31

When he rose to the surface, a cheer arose from the bluff above. His men caught sight of him immediately and from their scant belief and fervent hopes sprang cheers and jubilation. Their leader had indeed surpassed the hopes and expectations of their Angle kinsmen.

The helmet and armor were removed from his victorious body and they marveled at the mighty voluptuous orb and the golden hilt he bore with him.

Singing songs of praise to their leader, they retraced their steps from the waters of The Channel to the site of the resplendent meadhall.

The Angles were in the meadhall drowning their sorrows over the apparent victory of the sea-hag over the Saxon hero. Hrothgar and his queen, Wealhtheow occupied their thrones on the dais and matched the goblets of their subjects consumption horn for horn.

Beowulf and his band entered. The companions in full armor. Their leader still attired solely in codpiece.

In one hand Beowulf held Nodhung's hilt. In the other the giant mammary of his lover-foe.

Beowulf and his band bent the knee to the monarchs.

Hrothgar bade them arise and the Saxon chief addressed the king.

"O Lord of the Angles, behold the ransom I bring from the depths of The Channel.

"I would certainly not have survived my encounter with the dæmon who sullied this hall with her awful presence were it not for the protection provided to me by the mighty god Loki.

"I destroyed the wicked sea-wolf with the sword, Nodhung, entrusted to me by your trusted spokesman. The blood of the she-dæmon consumed the blade of the mighty sword. But I have brought back the hilt as a trophy of the battle I waged beneath the raging waters of The Channel.

"Another trophy have I also brought back to Heorot with me. It is an awesome breast of the one over whom I prevailed.

"With your leave, Majesty, I would nail it to the western wall of this hall."

Hrothgar gave the hero leave to mount the trophy on the wall. A task which Beowulf performed forthwith.

The assemblage cheered as they saw the hero standing before the trophy.

Gerda stepped forth and took Beowulf's hand in hers. And together, hand in hand, they left Heorot to the raucous cheers of the Anglomen.

The hero and his princess consort enjoyed great sport in each other's arms that night.

And in following days, weeks, and months, Beowulf took full advantage of the specialties of his sex-slaves who were ever available to him in his *leofhutte*.

In his most exuberant encounters, those with Gerda and even more intense, those with Feower, he found his satisfaction somewhat short of fulfillment.

He brooded about the lack he felt. He grew despondent. He began to lose his lust for life.

At length, the source of his malaise became clear to him. He was concerned that he would never again experience the most exquisite pleasure he had ever known – Sæwulf's embrace and its fulfillment in her love-death by his own fevered hand.

No carnal experience before or since was enjoyed with such relish, satisfaction, and such danger.

Had his dæmon lover prevailed, she would have killed and devoured him. By prevailing himself, he had been able to crown his own demonic orgasm by the higher fulfillment of killing her.

Within the depths of his soul the Saxon knew that he was doomed to truly love but once. And that love was for a dæmoness.

The truth Beowulf had to keep hidden deep within his heart until the day he died was that there is no satisfaction in life that is equal to the raptures of the love-death.

From the moment of that discovery, Beowulf was melancholy. For he doubted he would ever again confront a dæmon-lover.

He seldom was seen to smile again.

His band of fourteen began to talk of returning to Saxony. And Beowulf could find little reason to stay with his Angle hosts.

However, Hrothgar was deteriorating in vigor and health.

He talked to his counsel and admitted that he felt incapable of leading his people as he had been able to of yore.

After much discussion the king and his council concurred that if the Saxon hero were to marry Hrothgar's daughter, they would allow Beowulf to become king of Angle-land.

And thus his Saxon companions would become subjects of the island kingdom along with the Anglowarriors.

Beowulf was, indeed consulted. The concept of an Anglo-Saxon kingdom on the Great Isle was a welcome one to him.

And, in due time, Beowulf and Gerda became the king and queen of the Anglo-Saxon realm of Angle-Land.

Chapter Eight.
KING BEOWULF

Beowulf was the first and the greatest of the Anglo-Saxon kings who occupied the Great Island.

His reign endured for fifty years. During that half century he fought would-be invaders to his land – Frisians, Vikings, and Franks. He punished the peoples of the Great Isle who attempted to rise up from their subjugated reservations, – Britons, Pixies and Druids.

The great king led his warriors to victory time and time again. The Anglo-Saxons left countless enemy corpses scattered around the earth as feasts for ravens and as manure for the enrichment of Yortha, the Great Earth Mother's, realm.

From their conflicts, the Anglo-Saxons brought home numerous slaves.

As Beowulf increased in years, his beard grew white and furrows deepened on his brow. But his lustful enjoyment of the sex-slaves his subjects brought to him did not diminish in frequency nor intensity.

Yet his melancholy was not diminished. No lustful engagement with mortal women, slave or free, compared with the sheer delight, excitement, intensity, exhilaration or exuberance with the life-or-death intercourse he had shared with his dæmon-lover, the Sea Wolf.

It appeared that with Sæwulf's death all monsters had been removed from the realm.

And Beowulf mourned their absence.

The good king sought but one more experience of life-or-death copulation before he departed from life. One more pleasure-binge equal to the one he had experienced in his youth.

When he was in the fiftieth year of his successful reign, one of Beowulf's humble subjects was returning home from an overland voyage from a distant location. The sojourner was making his way over a desolate moor, anxious to return to the comfort of his home. Evening overtook the voyager as he was crossing a high barrow. Seeking refuge, he happened upon what appeared to be a sheltering subterranean cave.

The wanderer entered, intending to sleep in its protection before continuing his trip the next morning.

The sun had not quite set yet, and its fading rays revealed a sight that fascinated and simultaneously frightened the traveler. He found himself in a passageway stacked with treasures of gold, silver, precious jewels, and wrought objects of wondrous design.

But lo! Sleeping atop the treasure was an enormous dragon.

The voyager, Withergyld by name, beat a hasty retreat from the lair, but, having a flash of greed that overcame his fear, he snatched up a beautifully crafted gold wassail bowl and fled the cave clasping his booty to his chest.

The dragon had guarded her hoard for three hundred years. Content in her cavern and with the treasures she loved, she had no reason to go on dragonly rampages.

It was not as though the peoples who had occupied the land – Druids, Pixies, Britons, Romans, Angles, and Saxons – had been ignorant of the beast. Nor of the treasure she guarded. Her name was Freawaru, and hundreds of years before, she had flown down to the Great Isle from Ultima Thule in search of a treasure trove on which to rest comfortably. She tended to be a pacific monster who just wanted to be left alone.

Some time after Withergyld slipped out of her lair, Freawaru opened an eye to warm her heart at the sight of the beloved objects in her trove.

Her wassail bowl! Her beautiful golden jewel-encrusted wassail bowl. It was gone!

She scrambled through her treasures. She wondered whether perchance some of it had been swept deep within the treasure pile when she had stirred in her sleep.

But, no! Her beloved wassail bowl was not hidden among the shining treasures. It was gone!

Just because she was a peaceful, somnolent dragon, that did not mean that Freawaru was not still a monster.

She snorted fire. She bellowed. She emerged from her lair and emitted a roar that could be heard well beyond the shire. She soared up into the heavens and descended in fury on the first hamlet she spied. In a rampage of flailing claw and fiery breath she destroyed every habitation and devoured every living being in sight.

The dragon's rage continued unabated. Her violence spread throughout Beowulf's kingdom. Fear ruled the hearts of the Anglomen.

The people sought succor from their warrior king.

When Freawaru descended on the great meadhall, Heorot, burning it to the ground and gorging on the roasted warriors within, Beowulf feared that somehow he had offended the gods. Was Loki, the god of fire, demonstrating to him that Woden and Thor were displeased about something?

Or were the gods beckoning him to don his armor and demonstrate one more time, in his old age, that he was the fearless leader of a great people.

These thoughts moved the brave heart of Beowulf.

But underlying the resolve to seek revenge for the damage the monster had wrought was a more basic passion.

For deep down, he felt the gods had sent him a new dæmon-lover. One more passion which would be a life-or-death contest.

The stirring in his loins assured him that he had to prepare himself for the most exciting experience he would engage in since his battle-embrace with Sæwulf. He would have one more opportunity to experience the love-death if the monster was female. He felt in the marrow of his bones Lord Wyrd and the gods had sent him another female wight to encounter for the thrill of a life or death fuckfest.

If he was to confront a fire-breathing dragon, Beowulf knew he would have to go after her carrying an iron shield. Lindenwood would hardly fend off dragon flames.

Shield, weaponry, and armor. These he would invest himself with. But, as in his youth, he scorned a contingent of warriors. Since his naked battle with Grendel, he had relied on the strength the gods had granted him. And as with his love-battle with Sæwulf, he knew he could rely on his *membrum virile* as well should the opponent be of female persuasion.

Withergyld had kept the stolen wassail bowl hidden in his hut when he returned home. But as he became aware of the dragon's wrath he had stirred up, he feared that Freawaru could seek him out and punish him beyond even the sufferings his fellow countrymen had endured.

So, trembling with fear, he brought the fateful bowl to his king, trusting that Beowulf would be better equipped to deal with the dragon's wrath than he was.

Beowulf was pleased that the man had come forth with the booty. Here was a person who could surely lead him directly to the lair of the dæmon.

Beowulf assembled a squad of twelve worthy warriors to advance on the dragon's den. Withergyld made a reluctant thirteenth companion of the king. The finder of the bowl had no inclination or desire to retrace his steps to the moor and the burrow. He would have preferred to stay as far away from Freawaru as possible.

But choice had he none. So, shivering and trembling at every step, he reluctantly retraced his trail to the home of the frightful monster.

As the small band approached the barrow, Beowulf sat his companions down to address them.

He appointed young Wiglaf as captain of the band. The lad had demonstrated great courage in the most recent battles the Anglo-Saxons had engaged in. Of the thirteen men he had brought with him, he knew that only Wiglaf had the integrity and courage to lead, should the dragon prevail.

"I approach this confrontation with our nation's foe totally devoid of fear," Beowulf told them. "I accompanied my father onto the battlefield when I was seven years old. I have known war, smelled blood, and accepted the inevitability of death all my life. Now, as I approach the end of my life's span, I can tell you that death still holds no sway over me as I engage in the battles Lord Wyrd has thrust onto my path. There is no armor against Wyrd (Fate). So why does any man tremble before the acts he is called upon to perform?

"Whenever I had the choice to do so, I strode into the fray alone. The coming battle may be my last. But I have been in a hundred battles. And any of them also could have been my last.

"Whenever I had the choice to do so, I went into the encounter naked. To trust my unarmed, unarmored body in conflict with my foe has always been to me an unmatched delight.

"I would prefer to fight the monster in yonder lair without weapon, shield, or armor. But the dragon has her weapon of fire which I cannot withstand in splendid nakedness. So I shall confront her clothed in armor and protected by shield and sword. And the two of us shall face each other in the final throes of battle as Wyrd may decree.

"I send you men to yonder hill where you will wait with your weaponry to observe the fight of your king against the evil threat to our kingdom. I am the only one who can fight the monster.

"And either I will prevail, or I will die.

"Whatever be the outcome, men, remember this. You are Anglo-Saxons. Always conduct yourselves with bravery."

Wiglaf would lief accompany his king into the battle. But he knew that sometimes bravery can only be shown by following the orders of one's chief. So he led the band to the hillside as ordered and awaited the outcome of the impending battle.

Chapter Nine.
FAREWELL TO A HERO

Beowulf strode up to the cave's entrance and shouted his challenge.

"Freawaru, it is I, Beowulf, King of the Anglo-Saxons, who stand before your cave to challenge you. Come forth to encounter your fate."

For answer, a noisome, foul belch of flame emerged from the dragon's den, scorching the earth before it. The iron shield of the aged hero provided the necessary protection to his body.

There was a delay. Beowulf did not know whether the monster would accept the challenge and come out to engage him in the open or hover within, expecting him to brave the entrance to her domain.

Beowulf well remembered what the bards had proclaimed about the hero Sigord's battle with the dragon Vanir.

Vanir had emerged from his cave belching venomous fire. Beowulf hoped that Freawaru would react in that fashion. He had protection from that ploy.

Vanir, being male, had raised a leg and aimed piss at Sigord. Freawaru, being female, was not equipped with similar excretory equipment. Beowulf would not be subjected to the possible humiliation of being sprayed with dragon piss. There was some comfort in that.

Sigord had managed to manipulate Vanir into a position where he had been able to drive his sword, Nodhung, into the one opening where a dragon is vulnerable, frontally into the heart.

Every Anglo-Saxon had heard the story again and again, in prose, poetry and song.

The giant beast, Freawaru, sprang suddenly forth from her lair searching with baleful eye the human who proclaimed himself a king and who had the audacity to raise a challenge.

Beowulf drew his sword, aware it was not the Nodhung of old, but nevertheless knowing it would pierce his opponent-lover's heart if given the opportunity. With shield held against the dragon-fire, he took precise aim at Freawaru's vulnerable heart.

The dragon was aware that her challenger had precise knowledge of her vulnerability and slunk back into the cave instantly.

That first skirmish was a draw.

Beowulf removed his armor and his codpiece. He was determined to encounter this enemy in full splendid nudity as he had the two monsters he had subdued in his youth.

He stood without the cave and shouted insults at the foe within and dropped his sword at his feet.

Freawaru, though previously pacific in temperament, was still quite riled about the theft of her wassail bowl. And having a mere munchable human shouting insults at her was not long bearable.

This time, when she was ready to attack, she emerged from her den with slithery majesty.

She stood erect, her scaly breasts proudly pointing at her adversary.

At her sight, the king's magnificent resplendent cock arose into a phallus that caused the dragon's nipples to respond as the dæmon's cunt flooded with fragrant moisture.

Beowulf knew his desires, dreams and prayers were being fulfilled. The gods had sent him a dæmon-lover and the advent of a romance-binge that would end in a love-death for himself or for Freawaru.

Beowulf unexpectedly rushed straight at his monster-companion and impaled the creature's pleasure garden with his gigantic tool.

Both king and wight were thrown into a sexual ecstasy, totally overwhelmed by all rational sense.

The dragon collapsed onto the ground as her human lover pumped his heightened passion into her.

As the couple's dæmonic love thrusts approached simultaneous epiphanies, Beowulf, as a natural reaction to his passion, reached onto the ground, retrieved his weapon, and as they both climaxed, he thrust the sword into his lover's heart.

She, at the same moment, breathed ecstatic fire onto her lover.

And they expired in orgasmic bliss.

The legendary lovers lay dead upon the scorched earth.

In terror at the horrific scene they were witnessing, twelve of the thirteen witnesses fled from the scene.

Wiglaf alone, faithful to his liege, descended to the scene of the love-death.He lifted the charred lifeless body of his king from its resting place atop the dragon and bore it away from the scene of the old man's last conflict. And Wiglaf knew that, despite his death, Beowulf had been victorious.

Beowulf, during his long reign, had often told his people that when Lord Wyrd and the Norns determined that his time had come, he did not want his mortal remains sent to sea on a deathship.

As Beowulf had directed, Wiglaf bore his king's body to the Great Stone Circle (Stonehenge) that the gods had erected at the outset of the Age of the Gods, Asgard, which is the sixth of the universes supported by Yggdrasil.

An enormous funeral pyre was erected in the very center of the circle and the body of the noble king was placed atop the structure.

The Giant Circle could not contain all the mourners who gathered to bid farewell to the first and greatest monarch of the Anglo-Saxon nation.

It was Wiglaf himself who set fire to the pyre. The conflagration could be seen hundreds of leagues away.

As the fire consumed Beowulf's mortal body, Brynhildr descended from above on her horse Brida.

As the hero's brave soul arose in the smoke, Brynhildr gathered it into her arms and bore it to Valhalla to the wonder of the subjects of the newly elected monarch of the Anglo-Saxons, King Wiglaf.

The Saga of Wulfgar the Stalwart

Chapter One.
YOUTH

When Good King Knut (Canute) sat on the Throne of Angle-Land a husky male child was born to Osmund the farmer and his good wife Swerta in the hamlet of Acle. The hard-working couple named the child Wulfgar. He would be known to history as Wulfgar the Stalwart.

Osmond had previously begotten a son, Halga. And several years after Wulfgar's birth, a third son, Fin, was born to the farmer and his wife.

Lord Wyrd (Fate) sat on his throne at the root of Yggdrasil, the Universe Ash Tree. He dictated to his daughters, the Norns, the course that the newborn Wulfgar would follow. And, as the Norns do for both mankind and the gods, they began to spin out the episodes that would await the infant in the course of his life.

Unlike his older brother Halga, Wulfgar was, by nature, stubborn, disobedient, obstinate and horny. He was, also, fair of face and husky of physique.

Wulfgar was difficult to raise, but by force of fist, rod, and whip his father's thrashings caused him to be at least minimally manageable while he was young.

But when Wulfgar turned adolescent, at age thirteen, he bore fist, rod and whip with a sneer and had already grown sufficiently in strength to make even his father wary of much further physical abuse.

The time had come for the lad to toil for the family's good.

To this end, Osmond bade his son tend the flock of geese they kept on their farm.

"Son," he said. "You can't just sit around like a dolt. Get out there and tend to our flock of geese."

"*Shitte Fæder!*" (Shucks, Father) the lad complained. "Can you not perceive that I am a stalwart, not a milksop? Do you take me for a knave?"

"I take you for my son," the father scolded. "And if my son chooses to eat at my table and sleep in my hut, he will tend my geese."

Grudgingly, Wulfgar trudged out to the goosehouse.

And there, he herded the fowl in a way that gratified his lustful tendencies.

For he discovered one of the chief delights of a lively-minded gooseboy.

He chose a likely partner, held it by its neck and thus grasping it inserted his phallus up the feathered creature's *ars*. The goose would flap its wings, struggling up and down, thus giving the youth's member a lively workout.

Avowadly, the practice was more pleasurable for the youth than for the goose. Consequently the flock tended to grow apprehensive and shied away from its tender as intelligence spread of its tender's sporting nature.

In due time, Osmond decided that he would do well to find a different chore for his difficult son.

"So," said the perceptive father. "I perceive that you may be too stalwart to deal with fowl. Your very presence appears to disturb them.

"So I am changing your task from goose-chaser to shepherd."

Truth to tell, Wulfgar was growing weary of his intercourse with geese and had heard tales of the pastoral pleasures shepherds enjoy from their ewes. He was uncharacteristically compliant with his father's suggestion.

Perhaps the lad was growing out of his surliness. (Not very likely.)

With crook in hand, Wulfgar headed out for the sheep fold.

What delight he took in his work. He cheerfully serviced his ewes with a zest the beasties had never experienced from the under-hung, under-romantic rams.

When Osmond came out to check on his flock, he was content that his son was obviously successful in his new task. For the ewes were happily clustered around the shepherd. Albeit the rams *did* appear somewhat standoffish.

The time for the yearly meeting of the *Gemot* (Shire legislature) was at hand. Osmond, as a landowning freeman was a delegate to the assembly but his health was not up to the ride to Long Sutton. Wulfgar's older brother, Halga, was much more useful on the land than his younger brother. There was no question Wulfgar could be spared from his chores. And, truth to tell, Osmond would be relieved to have the scamp out of his beard for a while.

So a meal-bag was prepared for the young man. It was strapped to his saddle, and off Wulfgar rode to represent his father's interests at the Gemot.

The representatives to the Gemot assembled at the farm of Hathkin, who was thane of the shire. The group, led by Hathkin, set out for Long Sutton, each with his own meal-bag affixed to his saddle.

The band stopped the first night to sleep in the open under the stars, for the evening was balmy. Each man spread his blanket-roll on the soft sod and found sleep in his own way.

On the morrow, when Wulfgar went to his horse to remove the meal-bag to retrieve victuals to break his fast, the bag was gone.

He had no reason to suspect foul play. The bag most have fallen off the saddle sometime after the previous day's noon meal.

He spied one of the other members of the party, Eofor by name, searching the area, apparently a victim of the same mischance.

The two men agreed to join in a search for the missing items.

As they scoured the trail on which they had traveled the previous day, Wulfgar sighted Eofor stoop down and retrieve an object from the ground. He hastened to his side.

"What have you found?" he asked.

"Thank the gods," the fellow replied. "It's my meal-bag."

Wulfgar grabbed the bag right out of Eofor's clutches.

"You'll just have to go on looking," he ordered. "That is *my* bag of victuals."

Eofor made a grab for the bag but he was neither as strong nor were his reactions as swift as Wulfgar's. Indeed, as *Wyrd* (Fate) had long before decreed, Wulfgar was endowed not only with a handsome face and physique. He was also uncommonly strong and well-coordinated.

Eofor was immediately aware that he was outclassed physically by the young man.

"Then, I guess I *did* find your meal-bag," he equivocated. "I will just have to accustom myself to fasting until we get to the Gemot."

With that yielding statement, Eofor abjectly accompanied Wulfgar back to the spot where their horses were hobbled.

But when Eofor got to his stallion, he reached into a saddlebag and pulled out an axe. Displaying more agility than anyone would have expected, he hewed the weapon at the bully.

As agile as the man had proved to be, he was no match for his proposed victim. Wulfgar caught the axe-handle with his left hand, dislodging it from Eofor's grip. He caught the axe in mid-air with his right and drove the blade into his opponent's skull, cleaving it in twain. Eofor fell to the sodden earth splashed by his own brains.

The incident was observed by Hathkin and the others from a distance.

Hathkin approached Wulfgar.

"It is a dreadful thing that just occurred here," he told Wulfgar.

"This dolt stole my meal-bag," Wulfgar explained nonchalantly.

"At the meeting of the Gemot, that will not be judged sufficient cause for murder," Hathkin explained. "From my perspective, what occurred here would be more accurately be accounted a case of self-defense.

"Rest assured, the incident will be judged at the assembly at Long Sutton. If you are deemed innocent by cause of self-defense, there will be no penalty. Eofor's kinsmen will seek revenge of their own, of course. And will not rest content until they kill you. But if you are judged guilty of murder because of the alleged false possession of a meal-bag, you will be exiled by order of the Gemot.

"I would advise you to decide immediately whether or not you wish to proceed on to the gathering."

Wulfgar replied not a word.

He un-hobbled his horse, mounted, and galloped as fast as his steed would carry him back to Acle and his father's farm.

Chapter Two.
THE FUGITIVE

When Wulfgar reached home he recounted his adventure to his father.

Osmond had no sympathy for his unruly son. He would not even allow him in his house.

The only thing he would do for his fugitive son was direct him to a seafaring friend and acquaintance named Hrothulf who had a ship harbored at Harwich.

Osmund did not want to face the humiliation of having his fractious son apprehended on his land and exiled. Better to have him off to sea.

So, without so much as a blessing, Wulfgar prepared to ride off toward Harwich accompanied by a servant who was to carry Osmond's request to the captain.

Wulfgar's mother, Swerta, was concerned about her boy and managed to meet him before he departed.

"My bairn," she said. "Though you depart without blessing or means of protection from your father, know that despite your defects of character, honesty, or uprightness, your mother loves you anyway. So receive here your mother's blessing."

Wulfgar thought he could do very nicely without a maternal blessing. It had little value of any kind in his world. But his mother, kindly soul that she was, took his sneer for a filial smile.

"What's more," Swerta continued. "There are evil people out there in that harsh world, and you leave our land without weaponry."

She reached under her cloak and drew out a well-wrought sword that had belonged to her grandfather and had been passed down to her.

Now here was something worth eking out a smile for, and even a peck on the wrinkled cheek.

So, flashing a smile and pecking a peck, Wulfgar grabbed the worthy weapon from his mother's hand, turned his steed seaward, and followed by the servant, he was off in a cloud of dust.

Swerta, wistfully waving at the horse's rump, shed a tear.

It was the only tear shed by anyone for the departing wastrel.

When they reached Harwich, the servant pleaded Osmond's case to Captain Hrothulf. The captain was reluctant to accept the ill-tempered scowling youth, but because Osmond was an old friend of his, he allowed Wulfgar aboard.

The servant brought Wulfgar's horse back to Acle, leaving the stalwart with the reluctant captain.

The vessel was a merchant ship bearing traders in woolens, tin, gold and artifacts to ports in The Channel. There was a tradesman aboard named Hrethric who was accompanied by his fair, luscious wife named Ashhere. The couple was going only as far as the first port of call, Berck. After Berck, the ship was scheduled to stop at various ports along the way to its final destination, Sark Island. It was Wulfgar's father's intention that his son be left on Sark. That seemed to him distant enough from Acle to suit him.

Quarters for crew and passengers were located below deck. Wulfgar chose a private berth down in the hold for himself. No one else contested his choice. His obvious strength and surliness seemed to brook any dissent. Captain Hrothulf was content to allow Wulfgar's preemption of the space if that would keep the presumptuous young man out of his beard until he could unload him in Sark.

The young newlywed husband, Hrethric, was fair of face but inclined towards timidity, and was intimidated by the stalwart passenger who responded to every greeting with a scowl.

Hrethric's bride, Ashhere, had a very different reaction to the ruggedly handsome, beautifully muscled Wulfgar. Her brokered marriage was one thing. Her violent attraction to the lusty bruiser was another.

Every male on board, passenger as well as crew, was expected and required to work on deck in even shares with his shipmates.

Not so Wulfgar the Stalwart.

Wulfgar made it clear that he had no intention of leaving his berth for any reason. He was not available to bail. The hoisting, lowering, or management of sail would have to be dealt with minus his mighty hands and arms. It was savagely apparent that he would not lift a finger to assist with any nautical task.

Once launched, a good wind bore the ship south-east into The Channel. The ship was not well suited to rough weather and was inclined to spring leaks. The situation called for all hands to be on deck, not only to manage the sails and rigging, but also to bail.

Only two people were left below deck during the crisis, Wulfgar and Ashhere.

Ashhere feigned fear at the boat's tossing and went to Wulfgar's berth's door.

"O fellow shipmate," she intoned. "My husband is above on deck bailing out the incoming waters. I am left alone down here and am sore afraid."

It may not have been kindness or compassion which urged Wulfgar to open the door to offer succor to the distressed beauty. It is to be feared that carnality may have provided a more impelling motive to his action. But, whatever the impetus, the lovely young lady found herself swept inside the confines of the stalwart's quarters before she had even finished her plea.

Now that Wulfgar and Ashhere were together in the room on the wildly rocking boat, Wulfgar was left with a question of how to comfort his guest.

Both Ashhere and her groom, Hrethric, were virgins at their marriage. They knew what actions were expected in the bridal bed. And they managed to perform the traditional functions.

But, to Ashhere, the performance of her new husband was more tepid than she had hoped for. The performance of her husband's nude body atop hers was mechanically correct. But it lacked a certain ferocity. She had wanted to be taken. Instead, she had been merely serviced.

The brute who now had her in his power was more like an answer to a prayer than a threat.

Wulfgar's experience in lovemaking, up until that moment, had been limited to intercourse with geese and sheep.

His first realization when he found himself with a nubile female within his grasp, and an erection in his pants, was that his previous lovers, beasts that they were, were unclothed.

He would have torn the attire off his guest, but since she was already disrobing, he felt it more sensible to disrobe himself.

The couple faced each other in the wildly rocking room. They gazed at each other's nudity and their bodies gave testament that they liked what they saw.

Wulfgar's mind drew from his previous sexual experiences.

He knew what to do with a goose in this situation. Hold it by the neck and insert his phallus up the partner's *ars*.

He encircled Ashhere's neck with his huge hands. Alas, his partner was facing him and her *ars* was on the other side of her.

Wulfgar's fingers relaxed themselves spontaneously into gentle caresses.

The shivers occasioned in her by his action were a combination of fear and exhilaration. She was driven mad with desire.

Wulfgar placed his hands around Ashhere's waist, lifted her, and placed her on the floor on her hands and knees.

It seemed to Wulfgar that the sheep lovemaking procedure would clearly work better than the goose one.

Mounting her, he gave her the kind of wild, savage ravaging the young bride had hoped to receive from her husband.

Now that she and Wulfgar had become lovers, Ashhere felt her new paramour might benefit from a bit of genteel instruction.

Lying side by side on his bedroll, she taught him the oral pleasures of kissing and of breast sucking. She pleasured him with cock-sucking. She introduced him to the matrimonial position of sexual intercourse.

But as he learned each new sexual pleasure, his wild, animal adaptation of it gratified the young bride beyond her expectations.

When the storm abated, and Hrethric met his bride back in their quarters that evening, Ashhere was scarcely aware of his gentle coital endeavors.

And yet, her body had been the recipient of such madly exuberant experimentations in Wulfgar's den that she probably could not have born much more that evening than what her husband was prepared to exert anyway.

There was one more storm that disrupted the voyage before the ship arrived in Berck.

While Hrethric was on deck doing his duty, Wulfgar was doing his in his den with the fair Ashhere.

That second dalliance put thoughts of geese and sheep out of Wulfgar's mind for now. He felt that young ladies were at least as good as animals in the pleasure department.

He had found a real purpose for his life. The seduction of women would ever thereafter be his grand quest.

Chapter Three.

SARK ISLAND

When the ship docked at Berck, the newlyweds, Hrethric and Ashhere, left the ship to begin their new life on the Continent.

Ashhere left the boat reluctantly.

Wulfgar was happy to see her go. He'd enjoyed her, yes. He'd even learned from her.

But he knew the world was populated by females. He was not sure that in one lifetime he could ever get his fill of them.

He could hardly wait for his next seduction.

The ship proceeded on its journey. There were successful trading stops at such ports as Criel, Hever and Baruf. Wulfgar continued to refuse to be of any help on board. And Captain Hrothulf was content to leave the surly fellow alone, knowing he would be rid of him at Sark.

The last lap of the journey was from Guernsey to Sark. Midway across the channel between the two islands a tempest beset the craft which tossed it about like a chunk of flotsam. A giant wave raised the ship aloft and crashed it into the headland at the north end of Sark.

Unfortunately, the impact caused an irreparable hole in the ship's keel. Fortunately, all the passengers were able to escape to shore.

The shipwreck was observed by thralls of Thorfin, the Thane of Sark.

When they reported the wreck to the thane, he sent a contingent to the headland to help the survivors in any way they could. Hrothulf, Wulfgar and the crew members and the merchants and their wives were all brought to the thane's greathouse and attended to. Thorfin assured them all that when the storm subsided, he would send a large bark rowed by thirty men to rescue as much of the wares aboard the wrecked ship as possible before it sank.

The next day the sea was calm. And true to his word, the thane sent his thralls to salvage what they could. Much of the merchandise was lost to the sea, however.

The passengers remained a week at Thorfin's mansion. They dried out the wares that had survived and, along with the captain and the crew were ferried to Sesse on the mainland to fare on from there as best they could.

When Wulfgar arrived at Thorfin's mansion he was impressed not by the residence itself or its ornate furnishings. Rather, his eyes were enraptured by the thane's gorgeous wife Ursula and their lovely daughter Ingra. Then, when the servant girls were called to help the visitors to their rooms and to address their needs, his interest in Sark was even further enhanced.

Wulfgar determined he would remain behind after the captain and his crew and passengers had left for the mainland.

Wulfgar was surly and brutal by nature. But in addition he was wily.

In order to be able to seduce Thorfin's wife, daughter, and as many of the servant girls as possible, he took on a new, though temporary, persona.

Captain Hrothulf was amazed to see that his unpleasant, unruly passenger at sea had become a pleasant-faced, helpful, accommodating individual on land.

What miracle had the gods wrought?

Thane Thorfin was pleasantly impressed by the handsome young man and prevailed upon him to remain after the others left the island. His wife and daughter were even more impressed, and were made starry-eyed by the strong magnetic attraction exercised by the raw lust they detected lurking within that young visitor's robust body.

Wulfgar restrained his amorous ploys until after his shipmates had quit the island.

His first prey was Ursula, his host's wife.

There was no mistaking the interest she exhibited in his features, muscles and groin. Her husband, Thorfin, took no notice of his wife's stealthy glances. Wulfgar never missed a glance. And he managed a sly, beckoning rejoinder each time.

The Yule season was approaching. And, as was his wont, Thane Thorfin prepared to attend the family festivities at his parents' palace on the mainland. His father was the Eorl of Talburt and it behooved Thorfin, his youngest son, to keep in his good graces.

Ursula and Ingra chose not to leave their island at Yuletide, which was agreeable to the thane. He had liaisons aplenty in Talburt and enjoyed the liberty of amorous engagements there without the burden of attendant spouse and daughter.

Thorfin invited Wulfgar to accompany him to Talburt, but was informed by his guest that he was too much of a landlubber to face a sea voyage so soon after the distressing shipwreck.

Fire-breathing dragons could not have dragged the stalwart lecher off Sark while the thane was away.

No sooner had Thorfin's boat set sail for Talburt and the Yule festivities than Wulfgar took over full, undisputed charge of the mansion.

Ursula was accustomed to wearing nightclothes when going to bed. However, the night after her lord and master, Thorfin, had set sail from their island, she found that she was disinclined to do so. She told herself that it would be somehow more salubrious to sleep in the raw.

Once in bed, she lay awake expecting (hoping for?) the sound of someone entering her bedchamber.

She did not have long to wait.

The chamber door swung in and the buff visitor to the island had entered and closed the door behind him.

He was out of his clothes in moments and was lifting her out of bed in his burly arms.

Her heart had been beating rapidly at his entrance. But the feel of his great heft gave her an exhilaration she had never before felt in a man's arms.

Holding her firmly, he raised her lovely breasts to his mouth and suckled more voraciously than a suckling piglet. He had learned the pleasure of sucking from Ashhere, and now indulged in the practice with his native earthiness.

Having her in his arms turned his mind back to his early days when he tended geese. He had by-passed the practice with Ashhere because of the manner in which he had held her. However, with Ursula held as she was, he believed the technique he had perfected when a gooseboy could be employed. But only if his organ was well moistened.

Holding his lover aloft, her feet pointing toward the ceiling, her head aimed downward, he lowered her mouth down onto his male ornament. The goodwife was astonished and delighted to discover that her lips were encircling the glans of this amazing swain.

Once he felt his knob well moistened, he flipped her up so her head now pointed towards the ceiling and she was facing away from him. From this position he lowered her *ars* onto his phallus and entered her to engage in the goose inspired act. The lady was amazed and delighted. Never had she ever experienced such a sensation. Nor had she even imagined its possibilities.

She was being totally mastered by this masculine force of nature and was enraptured while being ravished.

When he had spent himself into her rear channel he laid her down onto her bed.

The dalliance the two engaged in there left the goodwife in a blessed daze.

She muttered thanks to Freya, the goddess of sexual pleasure. The goddess had been good to her.

Ingra, the thane's daughter, had been disappointed the night her father had left for Talburt. She had expected a visit from the hulk from Acle. He had not arrived, so she had to content herself with self ministration of her middle finger.

The next night, however, Wulfgar did not disappoint her.

He had been looking forward to enjoying the nubile young lady's body. He estimated that she was only a few years older than himself. But from the subtle indications she had given him since the first day of his arrival, he was sure that she was years ahead of him in sexual experience.

With Ashhere and Ursula, he had felt himself a novice in the seduction game. He'd had precious little experience with the one, other than with fowl and ovine creatures. Since then, he'd had a satisfying series of sexual assaults that had been most satisfying with the mistress of the mansion.

But, following his romp with Ursula, he felt a lack of knowledge.

What he most wanted to be in this life was a great seducer of women. And to reach that goal he needed to learn what kinds of embraces suited different kinds of the little dears. He realized that not every female creature would respond well to the kind of rough and tumble style that came natural to him.

So, uncharacteristically he had come to Ingra's chamber to learn rather than to dominate.

When he entered her chamber, he found Ingra lying on her bed, naked, her legs spread apart, and her right hand exercising itself at her groin.

He disrobed, lay down beside her, demonstrating that he was there as a student to learn from her. He engaged his fist around his own organ and pretty much followed the practice she seemed to be engaged in. Ingra took an interest in her bedmate's equipment and showed satisfaction in what she saw.

"Do you enjoy doing that?" she asked.

"It isn't exactly what I came here to do," Wulfgar answered.

"And just exactly what is it you came to my room to do?"

"To learn," he answered much to her surprise.

As each continued with his and her self-abuse, Wulfgar explained about his sexual experiences. He told her about the geese and the sheep he had seduced. And he described in rather graphic detail the romantic procedures he had employed quite spontaneously with the two human females he had encountered. Out of a quaint regard for his companion's feelings, he did not identify who either of the lucky ladies had been.

"So you see, Ingra," he went on to say. "I am practically a virgin. I have never learned what things please and what procedures displease the ladies. I feel that the more pleasure I can give them, the more pleasure I will derive for myself."

Ingra felt compassion for the unfortunate, handsome, gorgeously muscled and pleasantly hung fellow and agreed to teach him how to pleasure a woman.

She bade him desist from his self-abuse for the nonce and take close interest in her own sexual equipment.

"Had you been aware before," she asked, "of the boy-in-the-boat?"

Wulfgar allowed that he had not.

As she continued to entertain the elusive lad with soft strokes of her finger to her clitoris, he gazed at what she was doing with rapt attention.

"The sweet little organ gives very pleasant sensations to us females," Ingra explained. "But the 'boy' must be entertained with the gentlest of touches. We call the pressure the 'butterfly touch.' I would like you to take over the action from me. But remember, your touch must be no stronger than what a butterfly wing would be doing down there."

The stalwart young man attempted gentleness in his engagement with the delightful little organ that stood up so proudly in his little boat. But, alas! Gentleness was a mode he had never before attempted to acquire. The result was close to being a disaster.

Ingra pulled his face down to the spot between her legs and told him his tongue would be more likely to please her while lapping on the little devil.

Wulfgar was immediately an adept at laving the 'boy' with his tongue.

For the first time he knew the wonders of the scent that emanates from the female genitalia. He was intoxicated by its richness. And he was delighted in the spasms of his partner as he engaged his tongue with new-found versatility on the delightful clitoris. While he was pleasing the beautiful young lady, her fingers were engaged in the 'butterfly touch' over his own genitals. What a delightful engagement that was.

Nothing he had ever done with geese, sheep or the two previous human lovelies beat this engagement.

The healthy young couple continued in that fashion for the better part of an hour. They spent themselves in violent orgasm again and again.

At length Ingra felt it her duty as instructress to teach the lad a variation on the theme.

He was ready to add to his knowledge of technique.

"Now," she instructed. "As I lie here on the bed, facing up, I want you to get up on your hands and knees. On all fours. As though you were a lamb.

"That is the general position. But there's an important modification. Take the position!"

Although Wulfgar had never been one to follow orders from anyone else, he was only too pleased to follow Ingra in whatever direction she led him in her libidinous catechism.

"Now," she ordered. "Crawl atop me, your knees at my shoulders and your eyes looking directly down at my cunt."

Wulfgar found the directions baffling at first. But in due course he managed to hover over her, his genitals above her nimble lips while his mouth was directly above her cunt. He spied the boy-in-the-boat and knew that he would be descending to enjoy that fragrant delicacy. As he lowered his head down into the divine Y, he reflexively lowered his quivering appendage into his lover's awaiting mouth.

Because of his strength and stamina he was able to maintain this position as each slurped, licked, and sucked the other to his/her heart's content.

Thus was the second hour spent.

When they rested up from that encounter, Wulfgar asked Ingra what she would teach him next.

"That's enough instruction for today, Wulfgar," she told him. "What we have done for the past couple of hours will be sure to give pleasure to the females you encounter in the future. But know that in addition, you have an approach that every member of my sex adores."

"And what is that?" he asked.

"What you do naturally and instinctively," she informed him.

So for their third hour together, Wulfgar assaulted Ingra with the sexual rampage of a wild beast. There was no gentleness or concern as he tore into her nipples with savage ferocity, drove his hardon into her awaiting pudenda as ravenously as a male wolf on a bitch in heat.

He did not leave Ingra bruised, but her body had been well harried, ambushed, and assaulted.

She could not have taken much more of that. And she knew she could not bear such an overpowering masculine rampage very often in her life.

She had been taken above and below, in front and in back, squeezed and even pummeled.

She would cherish the encounter for the rest of her life.

And, although Wulfgar had never before been a great fan of having others attempt to educate him, he left Ingra's chambers very happy indeed to have been tutored in the arts of love.

The servants in the mansion, as so often is the case in great households, were very aware of what went on behind closed doors.

They could recount quite precisely what manner of trysts had transpired between the lady of the house and her guest. And they were equally well informed about the blow-by-blow encounters of the less than virginal activities of the young miss and the dashing stalwart.

The housemaids felt they had a few things to teach the handsome visitor themselves.

Accordingly Hocca, one of the lustier maids, approached the Anglo-Saxon stud with an invitation.

"Sir," she said. "Our master, Thane Thorfin, is away from our island, as you know.

"In his absence, his *leofhutte* has been left unoccupied.

"Whilst he is off to Talburt, and since you have taken his place in many respects, we housemaids were wondering if you might like to make use of it."

It seemed to Wulfgar that Hocca must have been dispatched to him by Freya, the Goddess of Sexual Pleasure herself.

"Does Thorfin's *leofhutte* come supplied with lusty womenfolk?" he asked hopefully.

"The master has me and two other enthusiasts attend him. Would you want the three of us, Sir?"

Wulfgar responded enthusiastically and set up the tryst with the three lovelies for that very evening.

However, Hocca had set up a condition.

"The master would be most displeased if he discovered the hut had been used by anyone other than himself. You must promise never to divulge that we let you in."

Wulfgar agreed avidly.

After dinner, Hocca came to fetch Wulfgar from his room and conducted him to a *leofhutte* situated a five minute walk from the mansion.

On the way he asked what he might expect at the hut.

"The master always has us three maids entertain him the same way. Indeed, if you are interested in anything other than Thane Thorfin's specialty positions, you will have to teach us how to perform for you."

"No," Wulfgar had to admit. "I am not interested in teaching. I simply want to learn. Whatever it is that the thane has taught you to do in order to entertain him is what I want as well."

Hocca's smile was enigmatic in its response.

The hut was modest in size but the interior walls were lavishly decorated. However, the room was bare of actual furniture.

In the center of the hut an enormous bearskin rug was spread out.

In each of the four corners there was an attached chain linked to a manacle. Wulfgar's interest was piqued. But his plan was to just let the girls do whatever they were trained to do.

He said nothing, and neither did the maids.

The three undressed him and then undressed each other. In the process of the disrobing, they ran their hands over his skin and over each other. The touching was in the nature of petting, and had the desired effect on all four.

Hocca, still silent, as were the other two, indicated that their visitor should lie down spread-eagle on the rug.

Wulfgar complied.

The maids then brought the four chains to his limbs and manacled him firmly at the wrists and ankles.

Wulfgar had never felt so helpless in his life. The feeling of vulnerability set up a series of tremors in his body that were erotically exciting. His member pulsated with a vibration unlike anything he had ever before experienced.

The blondest of the three lovelies bent over his groin and ran a moist trail over his genitals. He relaxed into the lovely sensation that enhanced the sensual pulsations that the bondage had occasioned.

Next, he was startled by an oiled finger entering his *ars*. He instinctively attempted to squirm away from the intrusion. To no avail. The finger ran up and down the canal with a caressing motion he found alarming and yet exquisite.

As that finger began to gently massage an organ up in that canal he hadn't previously known existed, the darkest-skinned of the three, Hocca, sat down on his face. Her squat did not cut off his ability to breath through his nose. And yet, she was perched so her anus was over his mouth.

His first reaction was disgust. But, to his surprise, the sensation rapidly morphed into extreme pleasure as the sweetheart at his prick encircled his glans orally, sucked deeply, and caused a tremendous orgasm.

As he spasmed, he found that his tongue was licking the orifice that covered his mouth.

While he recovered from the experience, the three lovelies made love to each other within his sight.

When he had rejuvenated, the girls switched places and he had a different maid at each position, performing the same operation, until he spasmed.

Then, after a respite, the three again exchanged positions.

When the tryst completed its third act, the maids dressed, unshackled him, and quietly exited.

He heard them giggling as they were going back towards the mansion.

As Wulfgar re-donned his clothing, he wondered whether or not the three beauties had just played a naughty trick on him. Although he never felt bound by any promise he had ever made, he knew he would never ask Thorfin if what he had just gone through was, indeed, something he himself had the girls do to him.

What he decided was, that as exotic and libidinous as the experience had been, he would only allow himself to be subjugated by another person again if his life actually depended on doing so.

So, for the remainder of the Yule season, Wulfgar was quite content to entertain Ursula and Ingra, and be entertained by them.

It was the happiest Yule the young man had ever known.

Chapter Four.
THE BERSERKERS

The Yule festivities continued on in joyous celebration until the approach of a Viking ship.

It was Wulfgar who spied it approaching the island from the open sea.

He recognized what it was from the nature of the shields that hung on the exterior of the boat from stem to stern. This was not merely a Viking ship. It was manned by berserkers, the most vicious, bloodthirsty and wildest of Norsemen who came from the sea to rape, ravage, rob, murder, burn and howl like savages while on their rampage.

When the craft was close enough to shore for Wulfgar to take note of the crew, he saw that it numbered twelve ruthless scoundrels.

Setting aside his native surly disposition, he assumed a hale and hearty persona to deal with the unwelcome visitors.

He strode down to the shore as the villains debarked.

He welcomed them jovially as he approached the leaders, asking them their names.

The leader, an ugly, scurrilous knave, introduced himself as Oslaf and presented his brother Ogmund.

"You have come to Sark at a grand time," Wulfgar told them. "What a Yule-fest awaits you here! The thane has gone off to the mainland and left his beautiful wife and daughter behind, as well as a houseful of luscious female housemaids. I know that you men will know how to entertain them. And the mansion is laden with beer and food enough to make us all merry."

The berserkers were delighted to hear Wulfgar's words and took an instant liking to him.

Wulfgar led the crew up to the door of the mansion and bade them enter.

Ursula and Ingra and several housemaids were in the hall, which was decked with Yule decorations. Ursula heard Wulfgar's voice welcoming visitors in to the mansion and called out asking him whom he was bringing in.

"Happy news, mistress," Wulfgar called back. "We have twelve wonderful guests who have arrived from the sea to pass the merry season with us."

When Ursula saw the vicious, scraggly crew bounding in, she was appalled. She could not imagine what had come over her handsome lover.

Wulfgar continued on in his jolly vein.

"I know you have been lonely, mistress, with the thane being away during this festive season. But grieve no more. One of this lively crew will warm your bed for you tonight. And another one will attend your daughter. And there are enough more here to keep the housemaids well entertained all night long."

Ursula, Ingra and the maids went screaming out of the hall, to the delight of the berserkers. They envisioned a riotous old night of fun ahead with those screaming bitches to ravish in due course.

Oh how the berserkers took to Wulfgar. A man they could admire and trust.

"Well, men," Wulfgar enthused. "Get yourselves out of those wet clothes, pile up your weapons there against the wall, warm yourselves by the fire, and I'll rustle up some beer to quench that thirst you worked up from all the rowing you've been engaged in."

The men laughed in agreement, removed their armor, piled up their weapons, and warmed their *arsen* by the fire as they chortled with glee in anticipation of the rape and pillage they anticipated ahead.

Wulfgar hastened down to the cellar and fetched up kegs of the strongest brew in the mansion to slake the berserkers' thirst. In fact, to drown it.

He placed the kegs on the table and provided drinking horns to the men who had rushed to sit at the great table.

The men drank voraciously, in huge draughts. And as they drank, Wulfgar regaled them with many a lusty tale. He interlarded his stories with suggestions that he would be delighted to join their band.

The drunker the men got, the more enthusiastic they became at the prospect of having this fine fellow as a member of their crew.

Wulfgar kept hauling up kegs from the cellar. And the berserkers continued downing it until they were roaring drunk.

Their boisterous talk turned to the women who had fled to their rooms. One scoundrel outdid the next on what he had in store for the woman he would do. Then they began to discuss the pleasures of gang-rape. Their speech slurred but the enthusiasm did not diminish.

Wulfgar steered the direction in another direction.

"Lads," he announced. "Rape is indeed a great pleasure. But do not forget plunder as well. In the treasure-hut down by the shore, the thane has casks of gold, silver, precious jewels, rare artifacts, and I know not what else.

"As it happens, I have access to the key. Why don't we all go out and feast our eyes on the loot before we indulge ourselves in ravishing the ladies?"

The idea caught on immediately. The crew arose and staggered towards the door.

It was true that Thorfin had not only shown his guest the treasure, but had trusted him with disclosure of where the key was kept.

Wulfgar fetched the key and got to the door leading outside ahead of the rocky crew. They were quite willing to be led to the plunder.

It was a short enough walk to the treasure-hut. The prodigious consumption of alcohol had made the berserkers immune to the intense cold as they traversed the snowy ground.

Wulfgar unlocked the enormous door and they all crowded in. When they saw the open caskets overflowing with riches, they became delirious.

While they were overcome with greedy frenzy, Wulfgar remained outside. He slammed the door and bolted it.

The berserkers were not immediately aware of what had happened as they stumbled drunkenly about in the dark.

Wulfgar hastened back to the mansion and called out to Ursula.

At first she hesitated, not sure of whether to trust him after what she had seen and heard him do in the hall previously.

She overcame her doubts and came into the hall.

"I have the whole bunch of rascals cooped up in the treasure-hut," he told her.

"The villains' weapons are over there in the corner. Have the male servants grab up what weapons and armor they can use against them. I need first-class weapons to go out there to fight the twelve scoundrels. What is the best available?"

Ursula brought him Thorfin's barbed spear, his short-sword, his helmet and his coat of mail.

Wulfgar rapidly donned helmet and mail, and with weapons in hand, rushed back outside.

Ursula called in the servants, telling them to grab weapons and follow Wulfgar.

Four of them appeared, armed themselves, and followed the hero. There were four others on the premises but they cowered away as far from danger as they durst.

The berserkers came to the realization that they had been tricked and trapped. With a surge of combined strength they burst a plank out of the heavily paneled door, howling like dogs in their anger.

As they burst through, led by Oslaf, Wulfgar came up with both hands and thrust his spear into Oslaf, running him through.

The spearhead was long and broad and as it came out of Oslaf's back the barb-ends went directly into Ogmund's chest.

The brothers fell down dead at the cleft in the door.

The others, enraged, trampled right over their dead leaders. Wulfgar set on them with his sword and his retrieved spear as they defended themselves with logs lying on the ground, or with anything else that came to hand.

Even though they were weaponless, each berserker was mightily strong.

Wulfgar slew two of them as the servants ran out of the mansion brandishing swords. But when the berserkers faced them with sticks the cowards slunk away into the darkness.

Altogether, Wulfgar killed six of the Vikings and the other six got to their boat. They defended themselves with oars and landed mighty blows on their pursuer.

Even though battered and bruised, Wulfgar ran two of them through. The other four got past him and ran off into the night. Wulfgar made out the silhouettes of two of them and slashed his sword through their necks.

But he was way too weary, beaten and stiff to attempt to ferret out the remaining two blighters.

He returned to the mansion where he was greeted thankfully by Ursula.

She led him to her room. And, sore and tired as he was, she ministered to him with soft touch and supple tongue in such wise that he lost awareness of his aches.

The next morning the people of the island went in search of the two berserkers who had escaped Wulfgar's blade and spear. It was late in the day when they were found frozen to death.

The bodies of the slain were born out to sea and sunk beneath the waters.

For the remainder of the Yule season precious to the gods, Wulfgar was very well taken care of by Thorfin's wife and daughter.

When the festivities at Talburt were finished, Thane Thorfin returned to Sark.

As he debarked, his loving wife ran to greet him and inform him of how her honor and her daughter's were saved by their guest. And also of how his treasure had been saved from plunder by Wulfgar's bravery.

When Thorfin got to the mansion he thanked Wulfgar, told him he would give him aid whenever in the future he should need it, and offered whatever he might want to take from the treasure-hut as his reward.

Wulfgar did not need to be burdened down with gold, silver, or other treasure. He said that all he wanted was enough gold or silver to last him during his voyage home. For he had determined to return to the family farm in Acle.

As Wulfgar boarded the boat that would bear him back to Angle-Land, Thorfin gave him the short-sword he had used to fight the berserkers.

Wulfgar bore the weapon from that moment until the day he died.

And as the boat pulled out into The Channel, Wulfgar pondered a question that would stay with him for a long time. He wondered if the three housemaids who had pleasured him in the *leofhutte* had really sat on the thane's face as they had sat on his. And if they had run their fingers up the thane's *ars* as they had his. Or had he, himself, been the butt of a mischievous prank on the part of the three lovelies.

He knew that he would never learn the answer to that question.

64

Chapter Five.
HOME AGAIN

With the faring silver and gold Thorfin had given him, Wulfgar arrived back in Angle-Land with enough wealth to live quite comfortably as he traversed the land from Harwich back to his ancestral home in Acle.

When he arrived at the farm, his father, Osmond, showed no great joy at the return of his surly son. However, the Gemot had since ruled Wulfgar's killing of Eofor an act of self-defense, so he did not block his return home.

For their part, his mother, Swerta, and his older brother, Halga, welcomed him with open arms. His younger brother, Fin, had grown up enough during Wulfgar's absence to be of real help around the farm. And he stood in awe of the returning brother who was actually in possession of gold and silver.

Osmond's health had deteriorated during Wulfgar's absence, and Halga ran the farm well with Fin's assistance. Wulfgar was as overbearing as always and refused to lift a hand to offer any kind of help to the family.

He used his time in pursuit of the lassies of the shire who were attracted by his physical attractiveness and by what they considered a sexually arousing masculine boldness.

The farmers of the area attempted to keep their daughters shut away when the arrogant returnee was in the neighborhood. But by wile and bluster, Wulfgar had his way with more maidens than any of his contemporaries. He had a kind of charm the men of the shire could not fathom but which appealed to many of the fair sex.

But conquest of female flesh was not Wulfgar's only goal in life. Physical domination over male strength also motivated him.

He made inquiries into who in the neighborhood was seen to possess the greatest physical might.

His brother Halga suggested the name of Audun, a young man who dwelt in Willowdale. Further inquiry on Wulfgar's part confirmed the suggestion.

Audun had not made any particular impression on Wulfgar before he had left for Sark. He vaguely remembered a blondish youth of gentle disposition. But the memory was quite dim.

His feeling that Audun had been somewhat retiring was confirmed by everyone whom he asked about the youth.

To try out his brawling abilities against the apparently gentle young man, Wulfgar set out early one day for Willowdale.

When he arrived at Audun's farmhouse he knocked on the door. When he asked if Audun was home a young farmhand informed him that he had gone to a near-by dairy to fetch victuals and should be returning soon.

Wulfgar strode into the house and settled down on a bench near the entrance to await his prospective opponent's return.

He did not have to wait long before Audun arrived carrying a bag of curds among other products.

As the young man came into his home with his arms loaded, Wulfgar extended his leg out from the bench tripping him. Audun fell flat on his face causing the curd-bag to break.

Audun leaped up, and far from the gentle response one would expect from his reputation, he exploded with rage. He looked around and faced Wulfgar, whom he did not recognize at first.

"Who the Hel are you?" he shouted.

"Wulfgar of Acle," was the answer he got. "Would you care to make something of it?"

Wulfgar was struck by how fair of face and how comely of body his opponent was.

Audun bent down, picked up the curd-bag, and pushed the broken bag full of curds directly into Wulfgar's surprised face.

The curds dripped down over Wulfgar's body. Wulfgar looked like a fool and felt more shame than if he had been wounded by the attractive lad.

He tore off his coat and shirt. Audun did likewise, aching to fight the bully who had tripped him.

They stepped out of the hall into the open space outside. Each was fighting mad, and set to grappling with each other.

Wulfgar gave of his all, and was met blow-for-blow. The contestants fell down upon the ground, wrestling with a ferocity that quite surprised the surly Wulfgar.

As they grasped, clenched, clasped and clung to each other Wulfgar was aware of a surprising sensation. He was springing an erection.

Not only was he aware of the alarming reaction. It was equally apparent to his opponent.

The two men separated, both embarrassed beyond measure by Wulfgar's very obvious physical condition.

Wulfgar was first to bluster a statement.

"I think we should consider our contest a draw."

Flustered, Audun nodded his agreement.

They re-entered the farmhouse and put their shirts and coats back on.

Wulfgar left without a word, not even brushing the curds from his clothing.

He mounted his horse and rode back to Acle.

Once there, he went directly to the sheepfold and had his way with a compliant ewe.

That night, once in bed, Wulfgar pondered the meaning of his reaction to the wrestling match he'd had with Audun. He came to no conclusions and fell asleep disturbed.

Chapter Six.
THE HAUNTED FARM

A wealthy man named Thorod lived in Shadyvale with his wife Gulda. He was the owner of more sheep than any man in his shire. He had an old, feeble retainer named Hnæf who lived in the house with them, who was their cow-keeper whose only job was to take care of the milch-cow. Not to milk it. Hnæf's hands had lost their strength to perform that task. It was Thorod's wife who took care of the milking.

Thorod had a serious problem. His property was haunted during the dark season of winter.

He had difficulty keeping a shepherd on the job during the season.

So he was delighted when a man named Glam showed up one day seeking work as a shepherd. Glam was a big hulk of a man, of ugly, uncouth, unkempt appearance. In fact, the fellow was physically repulsive.

Thorod told him he was in need of a shepherd during the winter.

"Winter sheep herding is to my taste," Glam answered gruffly. "But only on my own terms. I won't have others interfering in my life. I keep pretty much to myself. And I can turn pretty nasty if matters mislike me. Leave me to my sheep, stay out of my way, and I will serve you gladly."

"There is something I must tell you outright," Thorod explained. "There are those who deem this farm and pastureland haunted."

Glam's expression changed not a whit.

"I cannot be bothered by what fools care to think. I will work for you even if you believe such guff. But don't burden me with that kind of nonsense," the shepherd growled.

So they struck a bargain. Glam was to return to Shadyvale in the winter and watch over the flock.

Summer held sway over the countryside and no word was heard from or about the shepherd. But as autumn was veering towards winter, Glam returned.

With his crook, he took to the fields. That he raped the ewes was of little concern to his employer. That the flock clustered together when he whooped with his brazen harsh voice was a minor matter to Thorod. It seemed clear that the uncouth creature would remain on the job through the winter. And that was all that mattered to Thorod.

When Glam came to Gulda's kitchen, his demand for food was rude and gruff. He came close to assaulting her sexually, but cowered away when she warded him off with her butcher-knife. She detested him but did not fear him. She did not even bother to mention the quasi-assault to her husband. She was used to dealing with shepherds.

Yule-day arrived in due course. In the early morning Glam received his sack of food rations for the day from Gulda and trudged out onto the pastures to tend the flock, grumbling as usual.

It began snowing late morning and by evening a great storm descended on the area. Glam did not return home in the evening but it was impossible to go looking for him because of the snowstorm and the pitch darkness.

In the morning, when the storm had ceased, the men of Shadyvale joined Thorod in searching for the missing shepherd. They found dead sheep scattered about fen and slope. They came upon a place where the vegetation had been beaten down. It was as if giants had wrestled with each other savagely there. And amidst all this, they found a body. It was Glam's, beaten, bloated, and blue.

The sight of him was loathsome and caused some searchers to turn sick and others to shudder.

Giant bloody footsteps led off into the distance. No man felt any desire to follow them to wherever they might lead.

All agreed that the evil wight which had haunted the area before had killed Glam in a brutal battle.

They dug a shallow grave and piled rocks on the corpse. And many prayed to Hel, the god of the underworld, to keep the villain's spirit down below.

But when they returned the next day, the stones that had lain atop the shallow grave were gone. As was the body.

The ghoul that had been Glam stalked the area every night. It stomped the roofs of every house and hut in the vale, often with such violence that there were rents therein.

Some folk left the vale in fear and dread of the ghoul.

And people who lived elsewhere avoided passing through even if they had to go far out of their way to avoid the area as they ran their errands.

In the spring, things quieted down in Shadyvale and it was hoped that the hauntings were a thing of the past. And Thorod had no difficulty hiring and keeping serving-men. But as spring led to fall, the hauntings returned and the farmer lost his entire crew.

At that point a man by the name of Sturgot arrived at the farm looking for work. Thorod informed him of the hauntings, which did not concern the newcomer any more than they had Glam when he had first arrived in the vale.

So Sturgot was hired, and bearing his crook, he went out onto the pastureland and tended the sheep. And although Glam's ghoul continued to trod the rooftops at night, Sturgot was not intimidated. He simply could not imagine that wights bore any harm to him.

Sturgot was well-featured, polite, and agreeable. Gulda, who had detested Glam, was favorably impressed by the new shepherd. To the extent that when he was nigh and her husband was away, she welcomed him to her bed.

Sturgot was a much more skilled lover than her husband. The only problem Gulda encountered with him was that he reeked of sheepdip. But so had the other shepherds she had previously entertained in her husband's absence so she tended to think of the scent as a natural accompaniment to acts of sweet love.

Things progressed favorably at Thorod's farm until Yule-eve.

On that morn, Sturgot set out with his crook for the sheepfold. It was a cold day and snow was on the ground. But no storm seemed to be brewing and the shepherd had no concern.

When twilight set in, Gulda and Thorod awaited his return. Thorod was concerned. Gulda was next to herself with dismay that her lover might have met with harm.

The next morning, Yule-day, the men of the village joined Thorod in a search for the missing shepherd.

When they came to Glam's cairn, they found Sturgot's body, his neck broken, and every one of his bones smashed.

Sturgot was buried in accordance with the funerary tradition of the Anglo-Saxons, and in neither body nor spirit did he return to harm a soul. His spirit clearly now inhabited Hel's underworld kingdom.

But Sturgot's death initiated a new and violent rampage from Glam.

One morning Thorod heard a frightening racket in the barn. He dared not go in, fearing that the ghoul was at work. When the silence returned therein, he entered to find his faithful old cow-keeper, Hnæf, dead on the floor. His spine was broken and his body trampled on.

Thorod rushed back to the farmhouse and informed Gulda. They determined on the spot to flee with whatever they could carry with them. They had relatives in the next shire who were able to take them in. And that is where the couple went.

Glam's rampages increased. He killed all the livestock left behind. He raged through all the farms in the vale, destroying every living thing he could reach. Shadyvale became an abandoned community.

When spring returned, the hauntings abated. And many farm families, including Thorod and Gulda, returned to their homes. But when autumn returned, so did the hauntings.

Chapter Seven.
WULFGAR DOES A GHOUL

Wulfgar, back in Acle, was not aware of the events that were transpiring in Shadyvale. He sat glum and doleful, still not stirring to help his father and brothers with anything like assistance with the farm chores.

His thoughts turned constantly to Riverdale and to the fair-faced, comely-bodied lad he had wrestled there.

He had parted from Audun, brushing curds from his clothing. But he had left without taking his leave.

Courtesy was not a natural element of Wulfgar's makeup. But, in this case, for some reason unknown to himself, he felt impelled to return to Willowdale and apologize for having beat such a rude retreat.

He mounted his horse, and without explanation of any kind to his family, set off for Willowdale.

Audun spied his approach and hoped that the visitor came in peace rather than to cause mischief.

When he dismounted, Wulfgar made it clear that he had returned in the spirit of friendship and to perhaps enjoy a completely friendly wrestling match.

The two young men did, indeed, set to wrestling. But wrestling in a loving fashion which elicited genital responses welcome to both.

Wulfgar spent three days (and nights) in Willowdale. He shared his newfound friend's bed.

And during the conversations that filled their daytimes together, Audun informed Wulfgar about the hauntings at Shadyvale, two shires distant.

Wulfgar's spirit of adventure was stirred by the stories and he said he had a mind to go see those hauntings for himself. He had never encountered a ghoul and wanted to test his prowess against the unworldly creature.

Wulfgar bade his friend farewell.

The two agreed their encounter had been pleasant indeed. But further agreed they would not ever meet again. Their experience was one to be enjoyed but once in a lifetime.

And so it was.

Wulfgar set out for Shadyvale.

When he arrived, he was warmly welcomed by Thorod. Visitors were rare indeed at the haunted farm and Thorod and Gulda were a hospitable couple.

"Where are you headed, stranger?" the farmer asked.

"Actually, I came to visit Shadyvale," Wulfgar told him. "I have been apprised of strange happenings here."

"Happenings we have had aplenty," Thorod admitted. "If by happenings you include hauntings."

Wulfgar informed the farmer he was interested in hauntings and Thorod invited him to spend some time with him and his wife if he wanted to satisfy his curiosity.

"However," he warned the visitor. "I feel I must inform you. There is possible danger for you here. But whether you suffer any assault on yourself or not, it is certain that you will lose your horse if you stay with us. No one comes here without mortal damage to his steed."

Wulfgar scoffed that if something should happen to his horse, there were plenty of others to be had.

Thorod accompanied his guest to the stable where his horse was taken to a stall.

The farmer felt comfortable, then, in welcoming the rider into the house and introducing him to his wife.

The exchange of glances between Wulfgar and Gulda was lost on the host.

The three had a pleasant dinner, sat about and discussed many things. But they avoided mentions of ghouls, wights, or hauntings. And thence they hustled off to bed.

Wulfgar did not fall right off to sleep. He had picked up enough hints from his hostess to suspect that once the farmer was sound asleep his wife might find her way to the guest bedroom.

How right he was. And what a romp the two had. The skills Wulfgar had picked up while on Sark Island made him very welcome and well appreciated when Gulda was in his arms.

Glam did not visit the farm that night.

At breakfast the next morning Thorod commented that the night had gone well because Glam had not come riding the rooftops or breaking down doors.

Both Wulfgar and Gulda agreed that the night had, indeed, gone very, very well.

The visitor said he would like to stay with them for a while to determine if the ghoul was still around or if it had decided to depart.

Thorod encouraged his remaining. Gulda was even more extravagant in her encouragement than her husband.

The next night, again, Glam did not come. But Gulda and Wulfgar certainly did.

However the third night spelled a different story.

For when Thorod went out to the stable before breakfast the next morning to check on Wulfgar's horse, he found the door broken down and the horse dragged out into the open with every bone in its body crushed to bits. Thorod rushed back to the house where Wulfgar and Gulda were just sitting down to break the night's fast.

The farmer told them what he had discovered and all three hastened out to observe the wreckage and the slaughter.

Thorod strongly suggested that Wulfgar leave to avoid incurring the wrath of Glam upon himself.

"No," the visitor objected. "The wight has done damage to my steed. That I take as a direct challenge to me. I will spend tonight in the stable and await the return of the creature. Because having issued the challenge it is sure that he will return to confront me. And it is my intention to meet that challenge head on."

The rest of the day was spent with apprehension on the part of the farmer and his wife and a calm urge for revenge on the ghoul on the part of their visitor.

At nightfall, Wulfgar proceeded out to the stable naked in preparation for grappling with the spook. However, he was wrapped in his cloak to ward off the cold while he waited. He knew he would be unaccompanied that night by the buxom farm-wife.

He brought along only his short-sword as weaponry for the upcoming battle.

The stable was in uncouth shape. The wrecked door was widely ajar. Much of the side paneling had been knocked out.

Wulfgar had brought a lighted candle out with him which sent gloomy shadows dancing about the wretched interior of the building.

Wrapped up in his cape, Wulfgar began his lonely vigil.

In the darkest stretch of the night, the stalwart fellow heard ponderous footsteps approaching the stable.

When Glam trudged through the wrecked doorway Wulfgar stared at him full in the face.

He saw that the monster was enormous, shaggy, nude, and enraged.

Wulfgar slung off his cloak and bounded to his feet, facing the ghoul with unequivocal challenge.

Glam responded with a murderous roar and drooled down over his robust body.

Wulfgar held out his arms inviting Glam to attack. The monster leaped at the mortal, and Wulfgar shot through his outspread legs, grabbing him about his middle from behind, and bending his spine backward in an attempt to break it. But Glam was way too strong and Wulfgar knew his strength was insufficient to overcome the otherworldly creature in that way.

But the feeling of flesh to flesh and muscle to muscle evoked a physical reaction in Wulfgar he had recently felt when wrestling with his friend back in Willowdale.

With an unpremeditated thrust, he drove his turgid phallus firmly and with perfect aim directly up into the monster's *ars*.

Unknown to Wulfgar, the only method known to drain a ghoul of all his strength is through the act of sodomy.

Glam lay expired at Wulfgar's feet. He was powerless to so much as lift a finger.

"You have overcome me, wretched mortal," Glam growled. "And though you have won, you will lose. For I hereby lay my dying curse upon you. None can resist the dying curse of my kind. And thus you will suffer for what you have done to me.

"Up to the present stage of your life, you have acquired awesome strength. But it is only half the strength due you. My curse decrees that you will never acquire the rest of the might you could have had. And will never be a whit stronger than you now are.

"Until now, you have earned fame for your acts. Henceforth your acts will bring you naught but woe. You will be an outlaw, an outcast, and an exile from your land. You will find yourself alone and friendless. And loneliness shall be your bane."

Wulfgar felt the full impact of the curse fall upon him.

He grabbed his short-sword, and with one vicious swipe severed Glam's head and cut off the ghoul's cock.

Thorod and Gulda had heard the battle between the monster and their guest. But they had not dared leave the comfort and security of their home to see what was going on.

When quiet revealed that the battle to the death had ended, they peeked out the door.

What they saw was Wulfgar exiting the stable nude, carrying Glam's severed head in both hands.

They came out of the house and approached their guest. Closer examination of the burden held in his hands revealed that he had inserted the ghoul's genitalia into its mouth, from which it grotesquely emerged.

Wulfgar bore the burden to a post at the fence surrounding the farmhouse and set it there, staring madly out onto the pastureland as a warning to any wight who might consider coming there on a haunting.

The three mortals returned to the farmhouse. They dressed, and as dawn broke over the vale they sat down to breakfast.

After the meal, Wulfgar was satisfied that his adventure had gone well and he was ready to leave.

Thorod spread news in the community that the hauntings had come to an end due to the bravery of his guest.

He brought forth a horse as a gift for Wulfgar. Wulfgar accepted the horse, but refused gifts other than a token amount of gold and silver that could be easily carried on his ride back home to Acle.

Wulfgar left Shadyvale with a heavy curse on his head and a light burden of gold and silver in his saddlebag.

Chapter Eight.
SKOT-LAND BECKONS

When Julius Cæsar conquered Britain, he made it a province of Rome. The Roman legions occupied the province for four centuries. During that long period, various Germanic tribes made attempts to invade the Island, but the legionnaires had no difficulty rebuffing them.

In the sixth century, Rome herself came under attack and the legions were called home, never to return to Britannia again.

The Celts, who were the inhabitants of the Island when Cæsar had invaded were left to defend the Island against Angles, Saxons, Frisians, Danes, and other Germanic tribes after the legionnaires left. One of their kings named Arthur was successful in holding the tribes off.

But, by the end of the sixth century, the Angles and the Saxons managed to defeat the Celts, driving most of them north of a wall Emperor Hadrian had built or down into an enclave in the south.

The Romans had called the Celts by the Latin name *Scolti*, and the refugees who fled north of The Wall were known to the Anglo-Saxons as Skoten.

By the seventh century, the Anglo-Saxon kingdom South of The Wall was known as Angle-Land. And the kingdom north of The Wall was called Skot-Land.

In Wulfgar's day, a new king by the name of Duff ascended the throne of Skot-Land. King Duff was noble, worthy and generous. It was known that he welcomed noteworthy men to his court and that those who met his favor were well rewarded.

Wulfgar was perceived by his peers in Angle-Land as noteworthy for his strength and courage. His defeat of the berserkers on Sark Island and his conquest of the ghoul in Shadyvale were already the stuff of legend and song.

He believed that he might be well rewarded by King Duff if he presented himself at his court in Glasgow.

Wæscan (The Wash) was the harbor from which most merchant ships embarked from Angle-Land.

Before departing from Wæscan, Wulfgar bade farewell to his family. Because his father, Osmond, had become old, feeble, and bed-ridden, Wulfgar cast aside his surly antipathy towards the old man and attempted to play the part of the dutiful son.

He was not entirely successful in this attempt. Nor was Osmond very successful in hiding his glee that his bothersome son was leaving.

Wulfgar's leave-taking from his mother and his two brothers went off much better.

When Wulfgar arrived at Wæscan, he took passage on a merchant ship.

Berths had not yet been assigned to the passengers. Wulfgar, like most of the other passengers, repaired to the common room where they could order food and drink while waiting for the ship's departure.

As he looked over his fellow passengers, Wulfgar noted that some of the merchants had brought along wives and daughters to accompany them on the trip. Not many, to be sure, but enough feminine pulchritude to feast the eyes. As he scoped out the bevy, he noted that there were enough beauties who returned his gaze with yearning eyes to assure that the voyage to Skot-Land would be entertaining enough. He would have to insist on getting a berth below-deck that would accommodate a bit of maritime romance. He determined to make a statement there in the common room that would stem any resistance to his actions during the voyage.

Among the people in the room was a certain Thorburn who was a native of Wulfgar's shire.

Thorburn was jealous of Wulfgar's fame, but had kept himself distanced from him back home.

However, on board ship with his nemesis, Thorburn could scarcely keep his jealousy to himself.

In the ship's common room, under the influence of an excess of mead, Thorburn began to regale his fellow passengers with tales about Acle. Wulfgar could see that Thorburn's bravado would play to his advantage in intimidating anyone from interfering with his actions during the trip.

Thorburn told amusing tales about Osmond's miserliness, Swerta's lasciviousness, Halga's stupidity and Fin's laziness. None of the stories or claims were true in any way.

Wulfgar was insensitive to slurs about his family, because he truly did not care much about his relatives. Nor, indeed, about anyone else. But he saw that nevertheless he could use Thorburn's bluster to serve his own ends.

When Thorburn saw that he could get by with his slanderous talk without incurring Wulfgar's wrath, he began to make humorous, uncomplimentary and derogatory comments about Wulfgar's famous feats.

In his drunken abandon, he threw all caution to the winds. The passengers were appalled at what they were hearing. They were aware that the drunk blowhard was fabricating with abandon. They stole glances at Wulfgar, who sat drinking a horn of beer, his perennial scowl fixed on his face. He was listening to the string of insults without registering an outward reaction of any kind.

When Thorburn began to run down and started to grab for words, Wulfgar arose and faced the hector.

Displaying no emotion other than his customary sneer, he drew his short-sword. Suddenly, alarm registered in Thorburn's eyes.

"I believe my fellow passengers and I have heard enough of your buffoonery, you babbling nincompoop," Wulfgar growled.

He punctuated his sentence by hewing his sword at the drunk's head. And with a single stroke of his weapon he decapitated the man before the eyes of his travel companions.

The suddenness of the act astounded the witnesses, but did not appall them. Wulfgar's action and reputation inclined the timid to find justification for his ruthless act. And it excited a carnal twitching in the spirits of the romantically inclined females in the room.

Wulfgar stalked out of the room, nonchalantly wiping the blood from his blade.

He proceeded below deck and chose a berth to occupy. He returned top-deck and made provision for drink and victuals to be brought to his berth during the voyage. And he was not seen top-deck again for days. However he was seen by several of the passengers who came to visit his den. As it happened, those visitors were all female. And all came to him surreptitiously.

As the ship continued its way northward, the weather turned fowl. Not only was the boat tempest-tossed by gigantic waves. But frightful cold overcame the vessel and snow fell on it in abundance.

The steersman was forced to guide the craft for shelter into the Firth of Burnmuth.

On the opposite shore from where the boat anchored there was a guesthouse wherein was a group of revelers feasting and drinking in the welcome warmth from a blazing fire in the large fireplace. Whilst the storm raged outside with its snow flurries and frigid winds, the guests ate, drank, sang and danced.

Among that merry group were sons of a certain Thane Bodolf.

When Duff became king of Skot-Land, this same thane was his chief counselor and held great power in the kingdom.

His sons had joined a group of youths on an excursion to the south of the kingdom, to Burnmuth, where the foul weather had overtaken them. But where the merrymakers were safely and happily ensconced while awaiting a letup in the storm.

Wulfgar joined the passengers and crew on the deck of the ship as it lay at anchor on the bank of the firth. The cold was felt intensely because there was no kindling or fuel aboard. There was fear amongst many that they would all freeze to death right there in that sad, forsaken spot.

Wulfgar's shipmates saw flames shooting up from the chimney top of a building at some distance from the opposite bank. It was clearly unwise to unmoor the ship in such weather. And the prospect of freezing to death was an unwelcome idea as well.

There was earnest discussion whether any man aboard might be able to swim across the frigid waters, reach the building where the merry fire was raging, and return to the ship with fire-making material and fire itself.

Wulfgar remained aloof from the discussion but was brought into it by one of the less timid of the merchants.

"We know you to be the most stalwart man in Angle-Land," the chapman said. "You know the peril we face and what our need is."

"I know what it is you desire," Wulfgar snarled. "Fetching some fire from over there is not an impossibility. I hear you talk of need. But I have not heard a word of reward for anyone willing to undertake the task."

"We have many valuable goods aboard," the merchant responded. "I think you would find us very generous indeed should you bring us some tinder and fire."

Wulfgar looked over the crowd. Everyone was nodding his head and murmuring agreement with the chapman.

Wulfgar thought the matter over and concluded that it would be worthwhile to end up at King Duff's court well provisioned with mercantile supplies and enjoying the full favor of the merchants who were bringing needed goods to the kingdom from the neighboring kingdom below The Wall.

So he cast off his clothes, dove into the frigid waters, and swam across the sound.

He waded ashore, spied the house with the fire, heard the sounds of merriment within, opened the door and burst in.

There were twelve young people inside seated at tables and carousing in their refuge from the storm. A great fire was blazing in the fireplace.

When he stepped in, Wulfgar was covered with ice and icicles hung from his every appendage.

A fearful sight was he. He appeared too large to be a troll and too small to be an ogre. Whatever he was, he was a most unwelcome wight.

The men grabbed whatever they could find at hand and smote at him. A couple of the young men found firebrands and used those as offensive weapons against the intruder.

As a result, furniture and carpeting caught fire everywhere in the place.

Wulfgar fended his assailants off, and left the refuge-house bearing the fire and tinder he had come for. He did not know whether he had killed any of his opponents or not. He had what he had come for and headed back for the ship and his reward unconcerned about those he had left behind.

From the conflict inside, the entire building caught fire behind him, and the revelers were all burned to death.

When Wulfgar got back to the ship with the fire, the passengers were standing on deck encouraging his return but lamenting that the building he had gone to was burning to the ground.

The crew and passengers enjoyed the comfort of the fire Wulfgar had brought back. But they damned him for the destruction he had left behind.

Unanimously, they refused to reward him with so much as even a word of praise.

Wulfgar felt there was nothing he could do about the ingratitude since he wanted to arrive at Duff's court and could scarcely get there if he slew passengers and crew.

When the storm passed, the ship set sail again for the Firth of Forth and Wulfgar, cursing and mumbling all alone in his room held his rage within.

And at the same time, word was being relayed to Glasgow that Thane Bodolf's sons had been slain and immolated in a refuge house in Burnmuth. And it was told that the perpetrator of the outrage was on a ship headed for the Firth of Forth, and, thus, very likely would be landing at Grangemuth.

The ship did land at Grangemuth. Wulfgar debarked with his shipmates and they all rode into Glasgow together.

And once arrived in Glasgow Wulfgar accompanied the trade mission to the royal palace.

He waited in a saloon while the merchants entered into preliminary negotiations with the king and his ministers. When those discussions terminated, he was ushered into the audience room.

He bowed to the king who greeted him by name.

"You are Wulfgar the Stalwart, are you not?" the king asked.

"That is the name by which many know me," Wulfgar answered. "I have come to offer my services to you, Your Majesty. But, more. I wish to clear my name from an act of which I am accused but did not do."

"From what I have heard," King Duff replied. "I have already judged that you did not kill the youths down in Burnmuth. At least not wittingly. I suspect that some ill *wyrd* accompanied you to the refuge-house there. But I need to hear your version of the event."

Wulfgar told the king everything that happened as it occurred. He felt quite sure that even though he had, indeed, fought those in the edifice, that they were all alive when he left with his fire. And that the men inside had inadvertently started the fire themselves when they attacked him with brands.

"And therefore, Your Majesty, I offer my services to you, free of any guilt for the deaths that occurred at Burnmuth."

"Since there are no living witnesses to verify this story, are you secure enough in your mind to face trial by the carrying of hot iron?" the king asked.

This ordeal was acceptable by the kingdoms on both sides of The Wall. To prove his innocence, the accused had to remove a glowing iron rod from a fire-pit and walk three paces with it in his hand. His hand was then bandaged, and if, when the bandage was removed, the person on trial still had use of the hand, he had proved his innocence.

Wulfgar was secure enough in his innocence to readily endure the ordeal.

Three days later he was taken to the Great Circle of the North. It was a spot sacred to the Druidic gods and equally holy to Thor and Loki.

In the center of the Circle was a blazing altar fire wherein rested a glowing iron rod.

The interior of the Circle was crowded with people who had come to witness the trial. There was much discussion among the witnesses as they separated to allow the defendant access to the pit. They were amazed, one and all, by Wulfgar's strength and stature. And by the equanimity he showed when approaching the iron rod.

When he had taken only three steps into the consecrated space, a wild looking boy with a particularly ugly face, disheveled hair and wild mad eyes broke out of the crowd and glared at Wulfgar.

"You killed my brothers," he accused. "You are a bad man and the son of a mermaid. Whether you pass the ordeal or not, I declare that you are a murderer."

All this was said in a high pitched, raucous keen.

Having said his piece, the boy pointed his finger at Wulfgar, turned around and dropped his shaggy pants, pointed his *ars* at his victim, and farted at him.

Wulfgar drew back a leg and kicked the urchin in the *ars* with such ferocity that it lifted the lad off the ground and sent him hurling into the crowd.

It was claimed by some that the kick killed the child. Others claimed that could not be the case for neither hide nor hair of the grotesque scamp was to be found anywhere following that tremendous kick in the *ars*.

The interruption to the ceremony made it impossible to proceed and Wulfgar was taken back to the royal palace.

The king was dismayed at the ill luck that had befallen the Stalwart at the Grand Stone Circle of the North.

"You, Wulfgar, are a man of such strength and stoutness of heart that I would have you as one of my men-at-arms.

"But, alas, that cannot be. There is a lack of luck, an evil *wyrd*, that attends you. And therefore I cannot receive you as an acceptable man-of-arms into my service.

"You may leave my court in peace and remain in my realm all winter long. But before Midsummer's Day, you must depart Skot-Land or leave your bones behind here."

Wulfgar knew that Glam's curse had followed him into that kingdom. He was sure that the wild young creature who had appeared at the Circle was an imp from Hel sent in obedience to the curse that he knew would follow him for the rest of his life.

So Wulfgar returned to the Firth and caught a ship that set sail for Wæscan. He was anxious to see what adventure might await him back in his native land.

Chapter Nine.
ANOTHER BERSERKER

As Wulfgar came off the ship in Wæscan, a well-dressed man who was clearly of some means approached him.

"Do I have the honor of addressing Wulfgar the Stalwart?" he asked.

In his customary dour manner Wulfgar replied, "Maybe I am Wulfgar. What is it to you?"

The rich man was taken aback by the reply. He knew of Wulfgar, of course. His deeds were recited and sung by bards and minstrels alike. The deeds, yes. The surly nature of the doer…not so much.

Word had spread from the tale-tellers of Skot-Land down into the north of Angle-Land about the Slaughter at Burnmuth and about the Ordeal at the Great Circle of the North.

Wæls, for such was the rich landowner-merchant's name, had heard the tales. He felt he had need to employ such a fearless strongman. He had been aware that Wulfgar was headed for Wæscan and made it a point to be at the harbor when the hero arrived.

Recovering from his setback at the rude answer he had received from the new arrival, the wealthy gentleman re-opened the discussion.

"Excuse my abruptness, Sir," he said. "My name is Wæls, a landowner and a merchant of some means in nearby Baktun. I am prepared to reward a stalwart who would agree to reside at my manor house where my daughter Enid and I feel in need of protection."

Wulfgar had arrived back in Angle-Land without so much as a bezant in his purse. And the prospect of living in a manor house occupied by a rich man's daughter had instant appeal.

So the anti-hero set his mouth into an unaccustomed smile.

A goodly quantity of gold and silver coins was offered and accepted for Wulfgar to provide his services as protector to the persons and properties at Baktun for a period of one season.

Wulfgar accompanied Wæls to Baktun, a property that borders the North Sea. Wæls' lands were subject to visits by ships both friendly and suspicious. The need for a presence like his was obvious when Wulfgar arrived on the spot.

When Wæls introduced Wulfgar to his daughter Enid, the stalwart immediately knew his prime duty was to protect the blonde beauty from any ravisher, save himself.

Wæls had many errands to run in the course of his commercial enterprises. Much of the time, he was at the mansion at Baktun, of course.

But when he was away, he was comfortable knowing that his Enid was protected from any dastards who might come by sea, dock at his pier, and attempt to ravage her.

Now, with Wulfgar in the mansion, Enid was delighted whenever her father rode off on business. Because, although she dreaded being ravaged by a dastardly stranger, she delighted in being ravished by Wulfgar.

When Wæls was well on his way to commercial centers like Norwich, Yarmuth, Long Sutton and Thetford, Wulfgar donned a Viking costume complete with horned helmet.

He would go down to the docks and blast on a trumpet as though announcing the arrival of a Viking ship.

As he trudged up to the mansion, Enid would hide herself away in a safe spot, in an attempt to outwit the approaching marauder.

Wulfgar stormed into the mansion, swearing loudly.

"Be there women, mead, and beer for a sex-starved, thirsty sailor from Ultima Thule?" he bellowed.

His imitation was so brutally realistic it actually caused Enid to shudder.

He rampaged through the house, being careful not to actually destroy any of Wæls' belongings.

He always set out enough strong drink ahead of time so he would be somewhat drunk when he found the trembling, waiting young lady.

When he found her, (and she always made sure he did so without too much difficulty), he tore off her clothing, which was disposable anyway, removed his own costume, and assaulted her ferociously (sure not to leave a mark or a bruise on her).

Enid was raped, front and rear. She was forced to fellate him and swallow such emission as might occur. She was forced to receive floggings on her backsides (where the welts would never be discovered by another) and receive other such indignities as can only be appreciated by a female with an urgent need to be mastered by a brutish partner.

When Wæls returned from his business ventures, he never had a clue about the recreations his daughter and her protector had engaged in.

He was satisfied Enid had been taken care of.

She had been.

A berserker named Snækol came ashore one fine day when Wæls was at home. Snækol was not just one of your run of the mill berserkers. His fame as a particularly nasty piece of work was notorious in every port and inlet around the North Sea.

He rode his warhorse off his ship onto Wæls' docks.

Wulfgar, Wæls and Enid were strolling on the pastureland of the farm. Snækol spied them and rode directly to confront the threesome.

Snækol was an imposing sight sitting on his steed. His helmet was loose fitting with the cheek-guards undone. He was holding his iron-rimmed shield before him and was quite menacing in appearance.

He addressed Enid.

"You, Girl," he growled. "Hop up here onto my horse with me and I'll ride off with you and show you what a real man can do with a maid."

Enid shrank back behind her father and her protector.

Snækol next addressed Wæls.

"You, Old Man. Prepare to either get that whore of a daughter of yours up here onto my horse or get ready to defend her. Because I have a mind to rape her and I don't believe there's much you can do about it."

Wæls did not answer and a great silence hung in the air.

Wulfgar stepped forward and assumed a meek, even cowardly expression and stance.

"Look," he said meekly. "Neither this goodman nor I is skilled in fighting. We are men of peace. And the young lady is a virgin whose modesty should be honored and respected by a gentleman like you. So please return to your ship without molesting any of us. You will feel better for your actions as you do so."

As he was uttering those conciliatory words, he edged closer and closer to the berserker until he was side by side with the horse's flank.

The berserker began to roar with rage. He bit the rim of his shield gaping over it down at the mild-mannered young man.

Wulfgar grabbed the bottom of the shield, thrust upward with all his might, which drove it up through the Viking's mouth. With his other hand he swept the villain off his horse. As the berserker fell, Wulfgar drew the short-sword that always hung by his side and beheaded his foe with one swipe.

Snækol's shipmates observed the action from aboard their ship. They had no heart to engage with such a one as they had seen overcoming their captain and set out to sea with haste.

Wulfgar stayed on as formerly agreed, and at the end of the season prepared to go in search of new adventure.

Wæls paid the strong man handsomely and wished him well.

Enid wept as her protector rode away, fervently hoping her father could find another guard as skillful as Wulfgar. She never told her father what the skills were that she admired so in the departing protector.

Wulfgar earned little renown for his action against Snækol the Berserker.

His detractors claimed the trick he had employed had been sung about previous heroes and thus had no novelty worth incorporating in a saga.

Wulfgar attributed the lack of renown for his clever ploy to the curse of Glam.

Chapter Ten.
WOLFGAR THE OUTLAW

When Wulfgar was getting ready to leave Baktun and head home, a drama was unfolding in Acle.

There had been a feud between Wulfgar's family and that of another farm family across the shire. The dispute went back to an earlier time when the Saxons had defeated the Celts and were settling on the newly conquered land.

There had been squabbles about boundaries, fences, flocks and workers among the victorious Anglo-Saxons. There had been fist fights and, on one occasion in the distant past, there had even been a duel in which each participant had killed the other.

Wulfgar's father, Osmond, had died while Wulfgar had been away in Skot-Land. For reasons which are inexplicable, that death caused a man named Hygelac, a member of the feuding family, to take it into his head to settle matters with Osmond's son Halga.

Hygelac went to the farm that was by then Halga's, and beat on the door. When Halga opened the door to see who was there, Hygelac thrust a spear into him with both hands, running him through.

Swerta heard Halga's cry of surprise when he was aware of the neighbor with the spear. She ran to the door and saw Hygelac running away.

Swerta called for her men. They were unable to catch the murderer. There was nothing left to do but lay Halga's corpse out and bury him beside his father.

There was great mourning in the shire, for Halga was well-known and generally liked.

Swerta knew she could do nothing about her loss. For in a blood-feud, no punishment existed under Anglo-Saxon law. All she could do was await the return of her son Wulfgar. She knew that when he arrived back in Acle he would take care of his obligation. And when he did so, the cowardly evil Hygelac would pay the blood-price.

Nor was the death of Halga the sole calamity that had transpired prior to Wulfgar leaving Baktun.

Thane Bodolf was sorely disappointed by King Duff's decision to allow Wulfgar to leave Skot-Land without punishment. For he was convinced in his own mind that Wulfgar had, indeed, murdered his sons.

Acting as if under the authority of his king, he went south into Angle-Land and to the court of King Knut (Canute) in Sandwich.

He presented himself to Eorl Skapor, who was Knut's Master of the Witan (the Anglo-Saxon High Council).

King Knut was concerned at the time about a massing of Norwegian and Danish ships in the North Sea, apparently poised to attack Angle-Land. The king was hoping to gain support of the Skot King Duff in a military alliance against the threatening Norwegians and Danes.

Bodolf claimed to Skapor that one of Knut's subjects, Wulfgar by name, had cold-bloodedly murdered his sons. And further that the murderer had escaped King Duff's justice by fleeing south of The Wall.

He treacherously claimed he had been sent by Duff to Sandwich to plead that the villain be punished by the Anglo-Saxons.

Skapor called a meeting of the Witan and explained the happening at Burnmuth from Thane Bodolf's perspective.

Skapor was not concerned with the justice of the case. But he was very much concerned with gaining King Duff's support in the impending conflict with the Danes and Norwegians.

The upshot was that the Witan declared Wulfgar an outlaw. The penalty for his alleged murders was exile and a sentence of death by beheading if he were captured within the kingdom of Angle-Land.

Wulfgar was unaware of the two grievous events, his brother's murder and his own condemnation to exile, when he departed from Baktun.

He headed first for Hrotham, where dwelt a cousin of his named Grim. Wulfgar planned to spend a few days with the cousin before completing his ride to Acle.

When he arrived at Grim's home he was warmly welcomed. But he was also apprised of the unwelcome news about Halga and about the decision in Sandwich declaring him an outlaw.

Wulfgar did not bide long in Hrotham, for he was desirous to get to Acle soon in order that the scurvy Hygelac might be made to atone for his perfidious murder.

Taking leave of his cousin, the stalwart headed for Acle. He arrived there in the dead of night when everyone but his mother was asleep.

He entered the farmhouse stealthily and found his way directly to Swerta's bedroom.

Although her room was dark, she recognized Wulfgar as soon as he entered.

She arose from her bed, kissed her son, and spoke to him of what was on her mind.

"I have been awaiting you, son," she said. "I knew you would come here. Your brother's murder must be avenged. And no one but you is available to do what must be done. My son, Fin, is yet too young to be able to successfully draw counter-blood.

"You have been declared an outlaw so no more harm can befall you from the laws of our land, whatever you may do by force of sword, pike or hatchet."

Wulfgar assured his mother that she need not be concerned. Halga would be avenged, regardless of whatever risk there might be to himself.

Wulfgar remained sequestered in the house, unknown to the outside world, while observance was made by Swerta's thralls about where Hygelac might be found.

Word reached Wulfgar one day that Hygelac was on his farmland for the end-days of the hay-harvest.

Acting upon that intelligence, Wulfgar mounted his steed and headed for Hygelac's farm. He arrived there around noon and knocked on the door.

Women came to the door, looked him over with appreciation, but did not know or recognize him. He asked them where Hygelac was and they told him he was out in the meadow binding hay with his sixteen year old son Arnor.

Wulfgar put on his cheerful face and looked the women up and down in a way that caused them to feel shudders of lust. He then rode out into the meadowland.

The father and son had bound up a load of hay and were starting to tackle another. Hygelac had set his sword and shield against the load and Arnor had his hatchet with him.

When they saw the horseman approaching they went to meet him. Wulfgar was wearing his helmet, was girt with his short-sword, and held a great spear that had no barbs on it but had a socket inlaid with silver. He removed the rivet from the shaft so that once thrown Hygelac could not throw it back at him with any menace.

Hygelac recognized Wulfgar as he approached and knew very well what he was about.

He told his son, "I will go to confront that enemy who has come to kill us. I will approach from the front while you maneuver around behind him with your axe. As he approaches me, you move up on him from the back and drive your hatchet with the full strength of both your hands right between his shoulders."

When Wulfgar was within spear-throw of Hygelac he dismounted and cast his spear at him.

The spear swerved and missed its target. Hygelac picked up his shield and sword and moved in on Wulfgar.

Wulfgar had seen the boy circling around to get behind him so was aware of where he was. He spun around rapidly with his drawn sword and swung it with such force against Arnor's head that it shattered his skull.

While Wulfgar was thus engaged, Hygelac rushed at him and thrust his sword at him. Wulfgar parried with his buckler, thrusted with his sword, and with a downward blow connected with his head, spilling his enemy's brains all over him.

The women in the house saw the handsome stranger riding away, and from their description there was no question in the shire who had killed the father and son. And with general knowledge of the blood-feud there was not any doubt that the revenge of counter-blood had been enacted. So no law had been broken. Which did not mitigate the fact that Wulfgar still remained an outlaw by virtue of the Witan's edict.

Wulfgar rode back to the family farm and informed his mother that he had fulfilled his duty. She thanked Thor, kissed Wulfgar, and gave him her blessing.

They both knew he would have to depart immediately.

"Farewell, Mother," he said. "I will be pursued for the rest of my life, so mayhap I will not see you again. Hygelac's family will never give up looking for me to avenge their kin's death at my hands. Then Bodolf, who is convinced I killed his sons will harry me until either he is dead or I am. And King Knut's lawmen will attempt to hunt me down as an outlaw so long as I am in the kingdom."

"May Thor go with you," his mother said as he mounted his horse heading he knew not where.

He knew he would need Thor's help. Because Glam's curse had clearly brought evil wyrd upon him.

Chapter Eleven.
A TASTE OF THRALLDOM

Wulfgar the Outlaw raged across the countryside. He took whatever pleased his fancy from anyone and everyone. From rich and poor, powerful and powerless, Saxon and Celt. Should a possessor of goods resist Wulfgar's greed, it was a question of 'your goods or your life.' Sad to say, there were even those who made a poor choice when confronted with that demand.

The outlaw grabbed, stole, growled and raped.

It was generally agreed that he was a bad man.

With Glam's curse hovering over him, Wulfgar's anti-social tendencies were unhampered by any restraints.

As time went on, he let his guard down more and more. Since he had been able to take whatever he wanted, whenever he wanted, from whomever he wanted, he grew unwary of any resistance to his whims.

One day, in the area of Waltham, after having consumed enough mead to render him careless, he stretched out in the woods, completely relaxing his guard.

Some shepherds passed by him and, as did everyone in the shire, they recognized the husky brute. Shepherds had been no less excused from his rapaciousness than farmers, merchants, or noblemen.

The shepherds spread the word among the Waltham farmers that the villain who was terrorizing the shire was, at the moment, unconscious and vulnerable.

Thirty farmers gathered together when they had heeded the shepherds' information. They lurked in the woods, observing Wulfgar, attempting to discuss whether it would be dangerous or safe to accost him. His strength, when awake and rampaging, was too well known for any rash acts on their part.

They retired to a distance to discuss strategy. Everyone wanted to rid the shire of the outlaw. No one wanted to risk life or limb in the attempt.

The huskiest ten men of the group agreed to do what had to be done.

They went back to their farms and returned with rope and nets.

They circled Wulfgar and moved in on him. Two men bound his feet with rope. Four others pinned his arms to the ground.

Wulfgar awoke with a start. He jerked himself into a sitting position, throwing away those who would hold his arms. He flailed about so that three men were knocked senseless to the earth.

The farmers with nets approached him from the rear and captured him in their snares.

Wulfgar struggled fiercely and for a long time. He was scarcely easy to subdue.

But at length the group of farmers prevailed and Wulfgar was rendered helpless and made their prisoner.

The men congratulated themselves that they had captured the hellcat. But now a new problem presented itself. What to do with the malefactor.

They suggested that Garmond, who was acknowledged the best archer in Waltham, take the outlaw and keep him until Vermond returned from the Gemot (annual gathering of chieftains) in Sandwich. Vermond was the shire representative to King Knut's Gemot, which was currently in session. Vermond would know what to do when he returned.

Garmond objected. He really had no place to keep the brute in ward. And he needed every one of his farm-workers to be tending to their jobs. He had no one to spare to keep watch over the roughneck. And he did not see to what purpose his archery skills would serve in retaining the scoundrel until Vermond's return anyway.

One after another, the farmers refused to take the outlaw to hold until Vermond's return. No one wanted to feed him, ward him, or risk what might happen should he get loose and take revenge on his warden.

At last they came to a happy solution. They would construct a gallows and hang the blackguard on the spot.

Wulfgar listened to their discussion. And he firmly believed the gallows conclusion was the unhappiest idea his captors had come up with. But he could think of no way to dissuade them.

They were all handy men with hammer and nail and very soon had a good sturdy gallows constructed.

They had a fine rope encircling their prisoner's neck and made ready to hoist him up when a fine lady came riding by on her mare.

When they spied her, the men knew immediately who she was. She was none other than the lovely Greta, the wife of Vermond.

Greta rode directly up to where the crowd was gathered and was favorably impressed by the hulk of masculinity who was tightly bound in ropes and was festooned with an ugly noose about his neck.

Greta was a very stirring woman and one locally deemed even wiser than her husband. When Vermond was off providing his counsel to the Gemot, she pretty much settled all matters in the shire.

She descended from her horse and asked who the fellow with the thick neck was. The one sitting moodily in bonds.

Wulfgar himself answered her.

"I am Wulfgar the Stalwart."

"Wulfgar the Stalwart," Greta asked. "What are you doing there?"

"My lady," Wulfgar responded. "Everyone has to be somewhere. And, as you see, this is where I am."

"How very unfortunate," Greta observed. "You clearly are a robust, vigorous specimen of masculinity. It somehow irks me that these milksops have domination over you. If you are to be dominated, someone more skilled should take a hand."

Wulfgar told her he could not agree more.

"What price would you be willing to pay to escape having your muscular neck stretched to a swan-like length?" she asked.

Wulfgar informed her that no price would be too high.

"If you will swear by Thor and to Hel that you will be an unquestioning thrall to me for as long as it should please me to keep you, I will save you from yon gallows."

Greta knew that no Anglo-Saxon man would ever break a vow sworn by Hammer-wielding Thor and to the underworld Lord Hel. She did not know, of course, that the stalwart was also living under the curse of a ghoul. But even under such a situation, even the most miserable recreant's breaking of the vow would be unthinkable.

The gallows or the lady? A slow, ghastly strangling death or thralldom to a gorgeous, seductive woman?

Wulfgar had never had an easier choice to make in his life.

The net was removed from the captive as well as all the ropes save the noose around his neck.

The farmers were relieved as they watched Greta riding away, the hoodlum trudging along behind her, his noose about his neck, and the controlling end of the rope firmly gripped in the lady's delicate hand.

Wulfgar was tied to the lady by something much more compelling than that earthly rope. No force on earth could break an oath taken by Thor and to Hel.

Greta's husband, Vermond, was quite wealthy and the couple lived in one of the finest houses in the shire. When Wulfgar saw it, he felt that things could certainly have turned out far worse.

When Greta dismounted, she led her newly acquired thrall into the house, pulling him in by the rope that terminated in the noose about his neck.

She then informed him of the conditions of his thralldom.

"Take off your clothes. Everything except your harness," she commanded.

Wulfgar promptly obeyed.

"Now, get down on the floor on your hands and knees and look up at me adoringly."

That was an order easily obeyed.

"For as long as you are my thrall, you shall answer only to the name Dogca (Anglo-Saxon, Dog). You will not stand like a human being but will crawl around as you are now, or lie on the ground like the animal you are. You may not remove the halter you are wearing. I am the only one who is allowed to remove it.

"You may not speak unless given prior permission by me…Do not look away, Dogca. Keep looking at me adoringly. There, that's better. Now, if you understand what I have said thus far, bark once. If you need me to repeat it, bark twice."

"Woof!"

"Good Dogca. Now, because you were a bad Dogca before you were captured by those fools, you need to be punished and disciplined."

Greta went to a closet and brought out a leather whip.

"I am going to teach you who is your mistress. And to do so, you need to submit to my whip. Lie down. You may face the ceiling or the floor. I allow you some choices and that is one. Also, you may whimper when you are begging me to cease flogging you. No other sound, though, may you emit."

Wulfgar knew he did not wish to be whipped on his front side so he rolled over facing the floor.

Greta lashed out with her whip. The lady obviously was no novice with the blacksnake. She laid the thong heavily onto his back, raising welts.

"I will continue to whip you until you whimper," she told him.

An, twa, thre, feower, fif, six

Wulfgar's back bore six bleeding welts. He saw no reason to withhold a whimper. Great Thor! Enough was enough.

"That was very nice, Dogca," Greta purred. "No need to hold out until you're beaten to death. I am capable of continuing with my whip until stubborn little thralls die if need be. It would be a worse way to meet your death than on the gallows those fools had constructed for you.

"Now, because you took your discipline so well, I am going to allow you some pleasure.

"Bark once if you would like to engage in a good time. Bark twice if you would prefer to taste the whip again."

"Woof!"

"Good. Now I am going to take off my clothes. I want you to get back up on all fours again, stick out your tongue, and pant as I undress."

Greta was a sight to behold in her splendid nudity. And Wulfgar's panting as she disrobed felt more natural and pleasant than he would have thought.

Greta lay down on the floor.

"Now, Dogca. I want you to crawl over here, nuzzle up to me, and sniff at every part of my body you can reach with your nose. When I say "lick," I want you to lave the area you are sniffing and keep licking until I tell you to stop. Then go on sniffing again."

For the next four hours, Wulfgar was engaged in sniffing and licking his mistress' armpits, neck, naval, toes, arches, nipples, breasts and her clitoris. She then turned over and he sniffed and licked her back, including her *ars*. He was reminded of his engagement with the three housemaids on Sark Island who, in turn, had sat on his face, where he made lingual contact with their bungs.

Wulfgar gave his mistress pleasure all day, every day. He mounted her doggie style, he lay on his back spread eagle while she played with his equipment to her heart's content. There was no way in the world that he was not led to satisfy her insatiable lust, but always as her brute beast.

At night, he slept outside, nude and tethered with his noose about his neck. He ate scraps out of a dish, not using his hands but rummaging through the food with mouth, teeth, and tongue alone.

And he was given at least one beating a day, which he could bring to a conclusion with a demeaning whimper when he had had enough.

Greta had rescued Wulfgar from the gallows to keep her amused while her husband was off attending the Gemot.

She had only kept the erstwhile stalwart in thrall for three weeks when word reached her that the Gemot sessions had come to an end and Vermond was on his way home.

The day before his return, Greta gave Wulfgar the most brutal beating yet with her whip, bade him put on the clothes he had arrived in, and sent him on his way in great pain, but well armed. She let him have back his short-sword as well as a pike and a dagger.

Greta knew that once her husband was back, she would be the one to be dominated. It would be easier to take the attendant beatings and humiliation now that she had satisfied herself with having reduced the famous Wulfgar the Stalwart into her absolutely obedient submissive thrall.

Chapter Twelve.
THE GRIDLEY AND THE GIANT

Leaving Waltham and his thralldom behind, Wulfgar stole a horse and a saddle to carry him on to whatever adventure might be awaiting him next. He did not know whether the owner of the steed was one of the farmers who had captured and sought to hang him. If so it would have added a degree of pleasure to the theft of the stallion. However he was happy to be getting away from the town and shire alive and free.

He headed south and west, robbing a bit here, raping a bit there, murdering from time to time, and generally making himself unwelcome everywhere.

As he rode into Blackmoor he was of a mind to enjoy a bit of domesticity. But of an order devoid of thralldom and whipping such as he had last experienced as a domesticated beast.

To that end, he cast aside his surly and rapine persona and feigned a gentlemanly one which did not come easily to him but which he could assume when it suited him.

He stopped at a mead-house and whilst consuming a brew or two listened to the goodfolk of the community. He learned that the people thereabout were concerned about hauntings by the gridleys.

Of all creatures on earth, Wulfgar was most repulsed by those loathsome gridleys who dwell in nasty privies. He had never had an opportunity to do battle with one of those noisome wights. Perhaps he could engage one, make himself into a local hero, and thus find favor in the eyes of one of the local maidens.

When he left the mead-house, he rode about the area. And sitting under an apple tree he spied such a lovely as caused his heart to flutter. He dismounted and approached her.

"Fair maid," he said. "I perceive by your tears that you are in distress. I am a gentle soul, and perchance I can be of assistance."

The young lady looked up and took in the dimensions of the man. Gentle he might indeed be. But more impressive, he was of handsome face and was of beautifully muscled torso as well.

"Thank you, kind stranger," the fair maiden replied. "I weep here beneath this tree because I dare not go back to my own home. A she-gridley has been haunting it and I have no place to go to escape her."

Wulfgar felt that perhaps Lord Wyrd had prepared this engaging situation for him to allow a bit of carnal comfort to soften the curse he lived under.

He introduced himself, and found that his reputation as a rapscallion had not penetrated Blackmoor.

The young lady introduced herself. Her name was Hygd. And she lived in a two-room hut perched near Blackmoor Chasm.

Wulfgar offered his skill and brawn to battle the wight that had ruffled Hygd's composure, and accompanied the lass to her hut where he was invited to sup and spend the night in the entry-room.

Blackmoor Chasm is an awesome rift in the earth. It plunges down sharply to a great depth, with precipitous cliffs on each side. A powerful waterfall cascades down one cliff. And the river that rages at its depth is mightily turbulent.

Hygd warned the would-be rescuer not to venture too close to the edge, for the chasm had claimed the lives of many an unsurefooted wanderer.

Hygd fed her visitor dinner and bade him spend the night in the entry-room.

She retired to her bedroom and surreptitiously peeked through a crack in the door as Wulfgar removed his clothing, set his short-sword within easy reach, and curled up on the floor to go to sleep.

Around midnight Wulfgar was awakened by a foul stench. As the stink grew greater, nearly overwhelming him, there was a great din just outside the door to the hut.

Wulfgar sat straight up, anticipating that he might soon have a chance to engage with a gridley.

He did not have to wait long before an enormous naked she-gridley burst into the room with a tub in one hand and a butcher-knife in the other. The wight was out to slice open human beings and scoop out their guts into her tub to take back to her foul privy for a midnight snack. In her world, there was nothing tastier than raw human guts.

She peered about the room to see if there was any available prey. When she spied Wulfgar she rushed at him, her knife pointing at his belly.

Wulfgar sprang to his feet and wrestled the knife from the wight's grip. The gridley beat him on the head with her tub and with a quick upward stroke Wulfgar knocked her tub flying against a wall.

The stalwart grabbed the gridley about the middle and she wrestled him back. The struggle between the two continued for some time, since neither could manage a satisfactory purchase on the other's body.

It surprised Wulfgar that she was the stronger than he was. But fortunately she was clumsier. And he had the advantage of finer honed wrestling skills.

Everything in the room was destroyed as the two rampaged. The noise that arose from their grunting, cursing, crashing and growling could be heard for miles around.

In their struggle, they had broken down the entry door and were grappling about out on the open swale beneath the full moon.

Their bumbling brought them to the dangerous edge of the deep chasm.

The struggle had wearied Wulfgar immensely. But the intimacy of their skin contact had occasioned the rise of a noble erection on his part.

Aware of the effect that penetration has on wights like his antagonist, Wulfgar aimed his prick with careful precision into the gridley's cunt.

No sooner had he ejaculated into her than her enormous power drained right out of her.

She lay motionless and powerless on the brink of the chasm. And with a well placed kick at her prone body, Wulfgar sent the wight over the edge and she plunged to her death in the roiling waters fifty cubits below.

Nearly totally exhausted by his efforts, stiff and weary, Wulfgar trudged back to the hut as the light of dawn appeared on the horizon. He entered the hut and collapsed onto the floor.

The sight of her hero sprawled out on the floor in his stunning nudity aroused a passion in Hygd that would not be stifled.

With canny and supple manipulations with fingers and lips, she coaxed Wulfgar into a priapic agility to meet her need.

And, yes, she found him fully capable.

The following morning, when Wulfgar had fully recovered from the exertions of the previous night, he was ready for a further adventure.

He led Hygd to the edge of the chasm and the two of them gazed down into its depths. The gridley's body had been washed down to the sea by the turbulence.

At the chasm's depths, Wulfgar's eye had spied a cave whose entrance was somewhat veiled by the waterfall that cascaded down into the churning Blackmoor River.

He had brought a long rope from the hut with him and looped one end tightly around a mighty boulder. He threw the loose end over the chasm's edge and watched it sink down into the water below.

He told Hygd to mind the rope from the top while he descended to explore the cave.

With that demand he removed his clothes and with his short-sword in hand dove the fifty cubits into the turbulent river below.

Hygd saw the soles of his feet as he descended into the waters and lost sight of him at that point.

He dived to the river bottom and came up under the force of the waterfall. There was a rock jutting up at that point that he climbed onto. He shimmied his way up to the mouth of the cave which was not far above the water level.

The anti-hero looked in and spied a great fire inside the cave with a naked giant warming himself beside it.

When Wulfgar bounded into the cave the giant leaped up and grabbed a broadsword that lay at his side. The iron sword had a wooden shaft. The giant smote at the stranger. Wulfgar parried the blow with his short-sword, striking the shaft and smashing it.

The giant reached behind him for a pike he kept fastened to the wall. But as he reached, Wulfgar slashed at the giant's enormous genitalia severing them from the body. In a mad frenzy, the giant leaped out of the cave and into the rushing waters. Wulfgar grabbed up the genitals from the floor of the cave and threw them into the water after his foe.

Hygd saw the river's waters turn crimson from the giant's gushing wound. However, she could not discern the source of the blood-red stain and felt certain that Wulfgar had perished down below. She returned sadly to her hut and shed many a tear.

Wulfgar, down below, explored the cave. He found a large bag of treasure, gold, silver and finely wrought iron objects.

Exhausted from his exertion he spent the night in the cave.

The next morning, with the bag firmly attached to his waist, he climbed hand over hand up the rope until he reached the swale at the top.

When he entered the hut, Hygd rushed to him, threw her arms about him, and he made love to her with the brutal vigor that was his wont.

Wulfgar remained with Hygd through Yule. But after the holiday he got a craving to return to Acle to visit his mother and his brother and to discover whether he was still an outlaw and a fugitive. Or whether, perchance, his sentence had been lifted.

So, leaving the lady behind fulfilled and richer with the giant's treasure, Wulfgar set out northward for his ancestral home.

Chapter Thirteen.
FUGITIVES TO STAEP ISLAND

On his way to Acle, Wulfgar came to a crossroad leading off to Baktun. Recalling how pleasant his stay had been there and the rough jolly games he and Enid had played when her father was away from home on business, he turned his horse down that road.

He hoped that Wæls might be away and that Enid might be home alone. Oh, what games they could indulge in were that the case.

But alas! When he arrived, Wæls emerged from the door, delighted to see him again. And worse! Wæls was followed by Enid, who, in turn was accompanied by a male protector. Ah, well. There would be no sport that night in Baktun. The prospect of jolly games had been an idle hope.

Wulfgar was invited into the mansion, of course, and his presence was celebrated with a grand feast.

Wæls assured him that despite the unfortunate decision of the Witan that had declared him an outlaw, he, Wæls, still stood by him.

"You need not go into exile to escape the king's justice," Wæls assured him. "I know of an island just off the coast of Sortness called Staep. I was told about it some years ago when I was passing through Sortness on a business trip.

"It is an extraordinary island. Unscaleable cliffs rise up from its beaches. Atop those cliffs there is a very flat, grassy plateau. The farmers of Sortness keep flocks up there. The only way to get to that plateau is by climbing the ladders that lean against the precipices. So, since neither sheep-thieves nor predatory animals can get to the sheep, they graze there without need for shepherds.

"So, if you should need a refuge from the law, and if you were of a mind to, you could go to Staep Isle, climb a ladder, and be quite safe from pursuers. You could pull the ladders up to the top with you, lowering them only when you desire to descend. I assure you, all the king's men in Angle-Land would not be able to get to you there."

That was welcome information to Wulfgar. He thanked his host for telling him about the refuge, spent the night, and taking leave of Wæls and Enid, departed the next morning for his family home in Acle.

When he arrived at the family farm, his mother greeted him with open arms. His young brother, Fin, was now fifteen years old and saw his adventurous brother as a hero. He listened avidly to every word Wulfgar uttered in telling of the adventures he'd had and about his plans for the future.

"A goodman for whom I worked over in Baktun, Wæls by name, told me of a refuge off-shore from Sortness, where I would be safe from King Knut's justice and from Thane Bodolf's pursuit," Wulfgar explained.

He told about the sheer cliffs and ladders which made the Staep Plateau impregnable. It was clear that King Duff's kingdom to the north was not an option for him to escape to. The continental and island tribe-lands of Angles, Saxons, Jutes, Frisians, Danes and Vikings were risky choices as well. And Ultima Thule was clearly an impossibility.

"However," he concluded. "Even Staep Island is out of the question for a hunted man on his own. To survive there, I would have to have a companion to help raise and lower the ladders, maintain the fire, and manage other daily tasks and chores. Ideally, two companions would be even better. I believe three men living on the Staep heights could survive very well indefinitely. But, alas! I cannot imagine how I can possibly find one soul, much less two, who would wish to join me in that isolated life."

Fin piped up.

"Brother, I would love to go with you to that island. Would that be all right, *Moder*? Guslath already runs the farm anyway. He was second in charge when *fæder* and Halga were alive. And the farmhands are all very capable.

"What do you think, *Moder*?"

Wulfgar held his peace. He would be quite pleased to have his bother as his companion on Staep. But it was his mother's decision, not his, whether Fin could be spared from the farm.

Swerta spent some time pondering the idea.

She responded:

"It is true, Fin, that were you to leave with your brother, Guslath would manage the farm competently for as long as I live. And our thralls are fine workers, loyal and brave.

"That is, all except that lazy, good-for-nothing Unferth. If it is the will of the two of you to leave me and the farm, it will grieve me, of course. But I will not stand in the way of what I perceive as your destinies.

"But if you go, I insist that you take that bounder Unferth with you. That will relieve at least one care from Guslath's and my mind."

Both Wulfgar and Fin agreed that the addition of a third person would be helpful when they got to Staep.

Both Wulfgar and Fin were delighted at their mother's decision.

All three knew it would be dangerous for Wulfgar to linger much longer in Acle.

The next morning Swerta gathered together supplies she believed her sons would need for their journey and for their comfort once at Staep.

Before they set off, she addressed them:

"Farewell, my sons. I foresee that death awaits you at the end of this journey you set out on. It is impossible to flee from the fate Lord Wyrd has set for you. So I know that these old eyes will never behold either of you again.

"Live your lives bravely, and beware of sorcery. For it is a bane of all the gods save Loki.

"And may Thor's hammer protect you from evil."

Unferth joined Wulfgar and Fin then on his nag and the three men set out for the village of Sortness in readiness for a new life on Staep Island.

At length the travelers arrived at Sortness. A man dwelt there by the name of Hrothmund. When Wulfgar told him he and his companions were looking for a way to Staep, the man was reluctant to help them. He, like most of his neighbors, owned a share of the island. Although he, himself, did not have any sheep pasturing there on the high plateau at the time. But his neighbors did. And Hrothmund was not sure they would be happy about any visitors going to the island.

Wulfgar's saddlebags were heavy with the gold, silver and bezants he had accumulated in his life of outlawry. And he was able to offer Hrothmund a sufficiency of the loot to make him a faithful, lifelong friend and helper.

The three travelers needed not only transportation out to the island. They had brought along tools like hammers, nails, hatchets and axes. But they needed lumber as well with which to construct shelter. And firewood as well. Whatever they needed, Hrothmund was able to supply happily. For a price, of course.

Amply paid for supplies and services, Friend Hrothmund provided a boat, three thralls, and a full load of materials for the trip. So in the dead of night, under the light of a full moon, the rowers transported the visitors to the island, helped them unload their goods, and returned to the mainland with the boat.

Wulfgar deemed the isle good to behold. From the sandy shores the cliffs rose sheer from the beaches as he had been told. It was quite evident that no one could ascend the precipices except by means of the ladders that were propped against the cliffs. And the ladders could be drawn up or let down by the masters occupying the plateau at the top of the island.

During their ascent, the newcomers saw that the cliffs were full of birds, which would provide an abundance of meat and eggs. Once on top, they observed that the grassy land was filled with at least eighty sheep...possibly as many as a hundred. The three newcomers were very unlikely to ever suffer for lack of food.

When dawn broke, construction of their shelter began. The labor devolved upon Wulfgar and Fin. For Unferth was much more skilled at getting in the way than helping. And whenever he so much as extended an arm for assistance, the effort was accompanied by grumbles and complaints.

A good-sized hut was completed in three days. A worthy firepit was dug. And thus shelter, warmth and cooking arrangements were available to make life comfortable for the three refugees.

Next, Wulfgar deemed that they needed sweethearts to take care of their lovelife.

He felt he would have to teach Fin and Unferth the fine art of ewe-coitus. But he was assured by his companions that they had long ago learned the practice back in Acle.

So the three masters of the island mingled among the flocks and each chose his own sheep-girlfriend.

Wulfgar and Fin were delighted with their choices of romantic companions. Unferth complained and sulked that the brothers had picked off the prettiest ewes on the plateau, leaving him with a choice only of the ugly ones that had been left unchosen.

And so the three men began their new life on the island.

Chapter Fourteen.
SURVIVAL

Yule was approaching and the farmers of Sortness who kept flocks on Staep all went together on a barge along with some helpers to fetch some of their sheep to slaughter to sell for the great feast.

When their barge approached the island, the farmers saw people up on the plateau. The sight seemed bizarre enough. No one had ever known of inhabitants on Staep.

They landed on the sandy beach and lo! The ladders were gone.

The sheep owners yelled up to the creatures on the plateau asking who they were.

"My name is Wulfgar. I live up here with my brother Fin and our helper Unferth," was the resounding answer issuing from on high.

"How did you get there?"

"If I felt it was any of your business I would inform you," Wulfgar answered jovially.

"Those are our sheep up there with you," a farmer called back. "Send down the ladders and we will come up to bring some down to sell for the Yuletide feast. You can come back to the mainland with us. Whatever sheep you may have butchered up there is of no concern to us. We wouldn't think of asking you to pay for them."

"Thank you for your kind offer," Wulfgar shouted down. "But none of us has any intention of leaving here at all."

The farmers offered money, goods, or anything reasonable that the people up there with their sheep wanted, if they would just let them come up to re-claim their animals.

"No," Wulfgar replied. "We are happy with the way things are. Just go back home like good fellows and don't bother to come back out here any more with your unwelcome ideas."

The farmers could not think of any answer to this bizarre request. So they got back on board the barge, mumbling a bit, and returned to Sortness empty-handed.

The farmers could not think of any reason to return to the island to attempt to deal with the unreasonable chap and his companions who had taken over the island.

So for the next two years Wulfgar, Fin and Unferth lived in isolation from the world.

In that time the three men had slaughtered nearly all the sheep. Of course their girlfriend-ewes were safe from being butchered. After all, Wulfgar and Fin were not barbarians.

The shortage of mutton was not a concern to the masters of the isle. Seabirds and eggs were delicious, abundant and nourishing. But the dwindling supply of firewood was a problem to them.

Wulfgar sent Unferth down the ladder regularly to seek driftwood on the beaches. And so far the wood they had brought with them, supplemented by the driftwood scavenged from the beaches below, had sufficed for their needs. But the supply was beginning to run out. The problem was that without fire they would be doomed to eat uncooked birds and raw eggs.

Wulfgar decided there was only one solution to their predicament. Someone would have to get to the mainland.

The four mile swim there was hardly beyond Wulfgar's ability. And he knew he had left extra gold and silver with Hrothmund in order to provide for future needs. So he could get firewood from his friend and Hrothmund would have servants row him back out to his island with the fuel.

Wulfgar removed his clothing, descended a ladder and plunged into the sea.

He swam with all his might and reached the shore at Sortness after dark.

He was shivering with cold and made his way as rapidly as he could to Hrothmund's farmhouse.

Hrothmund, like his neighbors, had never had need to lock his house, so Wulfgar had no problem entering.

Hrothmund and his servants and thralls had all retired for the night. In the main room a fire still burned gently in the fireplace, keeping the surroundings pleasantly warm.

Wulfgar lay down on a rug in front of the fire. He was very weary indeed from the exertion of his swim and fell fast asleep.

Not long after dawn two milkmaids entered the main room with their pails of milk from the barn.

When they saw the nude hulk curled up by the fire they had difficulty suppressing their giggles.

It had been over two years since they had ogled the bruiser back when he came to the farm. And what an eyeful he was back then, even fully clothed.

It went unspoken between the two maids that on his re-visit, the handsome devil should be shown good old-fashioned Sortness hospitality.

They knew it was very unlikely that anyone would be entering the room for quite a while. On their way to the kitchen with the morning milk they had never ever before encountered a soul. There would be ample time for hospitality.

The lovelies disrobed. One lay down on one side of the sleeper and the other snuggled up on the other side. The warmth of the bodies and an instant awareness of the femininity that surrounded him caused an immediate erotic reaction to very pleasantly awaken the stalwart.

He had enjoyed the company of multiple ladies back in the Sark years before, of course. But he had been chained down on that occasion.

This threesome, he knew, would be a frolic of a different kind.

And so it was. With free use of his hands, arms, and mobility, and the playfulness of the delightful companions who had encountered him as he arose from his dream state, he groped, felt, kissed, sucked and licked one partner while being simultaneously entertained by the other. He entered one while the other gently massaged his balls. Then, with a short respite he was into another as his prostate gland was oh-so-gently rubbed.

In all, it was as pleasant a morning frolic as any of the three had ever before known.

When the maids retired to the kitchen with their milk pails, Wulfgar was in a cogitative state.

"Yes," he concluded. "A goose is all right. A ewe is better. A lass is better yet. But nothing in the world beats two lassies before a cozy fire.

He briefly toyed with memories of his time with Audun the wrestler in Riverdale, but promptly dismissed them.

In due time a male servant entered the room to check the state of the fire in the hearth. When he saw Wulfgar sitting by the fire he recognized him at once. He hurried to a cabinet and found a robe which he brought to clothe the guest.

When Hrothmund came into the room soon after, he greeted his robed visitor warmly, ordered that breakfast be brought in, and asked Wulfgar what he could do for him.

The visitor was provided with a boatload of firewood and two rowers to take him back out to his island.

The previous day's swim had been onerous. But, all in all, the stalwart considered the effort well worthwhile. He had not previously even considered the possibility of a cozy encounter with the two lovely milkmaids.

How sweet it had been.

Chapter Fifteen.
DEATH OF AN OUTLAW

One of the wealthiest farmers of Sortness was named Hook. He owned more of the sheep on Staep Island than any of his neighbors. And thus he was possibly the most distressed of any of them by the untenable situation that had now lasted for years.

Hook, like his neighbors, was a religious man. He sacrificed regularly and dutifully to Woden, Thor and Tugh. His wife was a great devotee of Frida. And, indeed, all the gods and goddesses were duly revered by all his servants and farmhands.

But, inexplicably, none of the gods of Valhalla had responded to his prayers to rid Staep of those rascals who occupied and dominated the island. And, worse yet, who had been living off the sheep that he owned.

Living in the woods that abutted Sortness was a very ancient crone. She was not an Anglo-Saxon. She was one of the few Britons who had not gone to the northern or southern kingdoms when they were defeated by the Anglo-Saxons.

Not only was she a Celtic Briton, she was a pagan. A *wicca* (witch, sorceress), a bane of the true gods in Valhalla. Her name was Nimue. And it was said that in the distant past she had been an associate of that devil Myrddin, the magician who had been so powerful back in the time of the British King Arthur.

In his desperation, Hook went into the woods to seek the help of the old witch.

Nimue had looked in her cauldron and seen there that the wealthy Anglo-Saxon farmer was going to pay her a visit. She detested the Anglo-Saxons, but was not adverse to profiting from their rank cupidity.

When Hook approached her hovel, leading his horse by the reins, Nimue was seated in a clearing, watching over a cauldron that was bubbling over a raging fire.

The hideous old lady was mumbling invocations and curses over her brew.

When Hook approached, she cackled and winked at him.

"I know why you have come to see me, Saxon swine," she spit out at him. "You seek my magic to rid the cliff-protecting isle of its outlaws."

"Exactly so," Hook readily agreed.

"I can cause great harm to the interlopers," she told him. "There are three of them. The leader is an outlaw of prodigious strength. He cannot be overcome unless severely self-wounded. His brother is with him. He can be successfully assailed only while defending the great outlaw. The third member is a great fool you will be able to destroy easily enough without my assistance."

"It is your help that I seek," Hook replied needlessly.

"If I perform my wycca magic to your benefit, I must have your promise, sworn to your god Hel, that you will have your people construct a sturdy stone house for me here in the woods. That I will be supplied with a butchered sheep and a pig every day. And that no vile Anglo-Saxon will ever disturb my peace again so long as I live."

"Agreed," Hook replied without hesitation.

Nimue cackled her pleasure.

"Fine, then," she said. "Take me to the shore and let us commence at once."

The farmer hoisted the crone onto his horse and leading it by the reins brought her into Sortness and thence to the seashore.

Nimue and Hook stood on the shore looking out to sea at Staep Island.

"The first thing you have to do is take me out to the island," the crone told him. "While I am hidden from the outlaw's sight, you must attract his attention and engage in a quarrel with him. I can judge while watching him what manner of man he is and accordingly what kind of curse to cast upon him."

Hook set a ten-oared boat to sea holding him, Nimue, and eleven thralls.

When Wulfgar and Fin saw the boat approach they hauled up the ladders.

As the boat got within shouting distance, Wulfgar yelled, "Go away, Fool. We have nothing to discuss."

"If you don't leave that island," Hook shouted back. "It will go hard with you. Because I have my ways to force you off."

"The threat of a desperate man," Wulfgar responded. "I am here. And here will I remain until the day I die."

"You have spoken," the farmer shouted back. "And I will hasten the day of your death if you do not capitulate."

Nimue lay in the stern of the boat with a blanket covering her so she could not be seen. But she could manipulate the covering to observe the man she planned to harm.

Her high piercing voice assailed him from beneath her covers.

"Say that you refuse the offer of the goodman whom you hear, Stalwart One. And I warn you that the curse of Wycca will befall you."

Wulfgar was amazed, and somewhat chilled to hear the sounds emerging from the craft.

He and Fin well remembered the parting words of their mother. *Live your lives bravely and beware of sorcery.*

Fin said, "I deem that an ill omen."

Wulfgar could not hold back his anger and shouted down from his height.

"The curses of Hel betake you, Wight!"

With those wrathful words he picked up a large stone and hurled it down onto the boat. It smote the witch's covering.

A blood-curdling shriek keened out from the sorceress for the heavy stone had landed on her thigh and broke it.

Fin looked at Wulfgar in horror.

"I wish you had not done that, Brother."

Wulfgar scoffed.

"Do not blame me, Fin. The sorceress wills to do us harm. It is only right that I pay her back with whatever pain I can inflict."

Hook was taken aback by what had happened to the crone and bade his oarsmen beat a hasty retreat back to the mainland shore.

All the way back Nimue was issuing curses laced with promises of revenge for the physical pain the stout outlaw had inflicted on her.

Once ashore, Hook had the witch taken back home to her hovel. And there she abode a month by the moon as the broken bone mended. And once mended she was avid to wreak her revenge on the Anglo-Saxon devils atop the cliff-walled island.

When Hook came to Nimue's hovel after her healing, she hobbled next to him through the paths she knew in the dark woods.

They happened upon a toppled tree whose stump was wholly above ground. The base of the stump had been lightening struck. This finding was exactly what the teachings of Wycca ordained for the task ahead.

The stump was sawed off from the tree by Hook's servants and hauled to the clearing in front of Nimue's hut.

With a ritual knife she cut a vein in Hooks arm and caught a gobletful of his blood. She then added an equal amount of her own blood and spread the mixture over the blackened base of the stump. When the blood dried she carved mystic wyccan symbols over the surface.

On the night of the full moon she danced around the charmed stump in the silver moonlight, naked. Clockwise and widdershins she gyrated, hurling imprecations and magic formulae at the instrument of her revenge.

The next night, Hook's men bore the uprooted stump, as large as a man might bear upon his shoulder, to the shore.

With the bright moonbeams sparkling on the waters, Nimue cast a final spell on the stump that it should float out to the shore of Staep Island.

And as she had directed, the anointed stump was hurled into the awaiting waves and born out to sea in the very direction of the appointed island.

Unferth always grumbled and felt he was misused when he was sent down the ladder to scrounge for driftwood. The stump he had just found down on the sands was unwieldy to haul up the ladder. But he saw Fin peering down at him from up above and knew he'd have to lug the blasted thing back up or get a beating from Wulfgar.

So he sighed and climbed the ladder cursing loudly with the heavy firewood on his shoulder.

When he got up to the plateau he trudged heavily over to the woodpile and threw it down with a loud thump.

The stump sat there for several days drying out.

When Wulfgar deemed it dry enough to hack, he took his axe out to rend the wood into useable sizes and shapes.

He hefted his axe high into the air. As he did so, Unferth was sniveling to Fin about how abused he was by all the work he had to do and how unappreciated he was.

Peeved at the complainer, Wulfgar smote down heavily with both hands on the axe-handle, causing a clumsy stroke.

The axe did not contact the stump straight on. It caromed off the wood and sliced into his right leg, delivering a deep ugly wound through to the bone.

Both Wulfgar and Fin believed immediately that the witch's curse had been fulfilled with that stroke.

Unferth had not a clue about the significance of what had happened. And secretly he was glad the big bully had his comeuppance.

Fin bound the wound and made Wulfgar lie down.

Wulfgar told Unferth that it was now particularly important that the ladders be watched all day long and pulled up in the evening. Because if Hook and his men should come to the island, he could not fend them off in his condition.

Unferth promised that he would carry out his important responsibilities perfectly.

The weather became stormier day by day. The north wind blew colder and colder. And every evening Wulfgar asked if the ladders had been drawn up.

And Unferth, as much as he hated to go out into the beastly weather, trudged out to do his job rather than take a beating from his wounded taskmaster.

But Wulfgar's wound was not healing well. The pain increased. The gash began to gather ugly matter and the lips of the wound turned out rather than knitting together.

Fin attended his brother day and night and did everything he could. But, in fact, there really was very little he could do and he despaired of Wulfgar's life.

While Wulfgar's condition worsened, Hook's confidence in Nimue's magic increased.

He set about gathering a force to sail out to Staep to attempt an attack on the interlopers who had hunkered down there for far too long a time.

Twelve of his fellow farmers were willing to take up arms to attempt to re-take control of the island with its ideal pasturage that had been usurped by the great outlaw and his two followers.

The band of twelve, led by Hook, set out to sea in foul weather. But once well launched, the wind abated and gently carried the craft safely to the sandy shore of the island at dusk.

Wulfgar had, by then, become so ill he could not stand. Fin sat beside him and dressed his wounds as needed.

Unferth was sent out into the cold to tend the ladders. He grumbled to himself every step of the way as he approached the cliff-sides.

"They're both so mean to me," he groaned to himself. "You don't see either of them coming out to help. That mean muscleman pretends he's too sick from that wound he has to do anything himself. And that no-good brother of his won't stir from his side. And no one appreciates poor Unferth."

When he got to the ladders he was in full revolt against his thralldom.

"Make me draw up the ladders, will they? I'll draw them up when I feel like it, I will."

And with this rebellious thought in mind Unferth lay down to watch out over the channel towards the mainland. And, still in his funk, he drowsed off into a nice nap.

As Hook's boat approached the island the members of the war party could see that the ladders were not drawn up. Nor were they guarded from above.

Quietly the war party ascended the ladders and looked around the plateau. They saw a man lying on the ground. Then they heard him snoring.

Hook wanted to make sure the fool would not awake and warn his companions of the invasion so with on bold stroke of his sword he severed the thrall's head from its shoulders.

The band approached the hut stealthily. Hook listened at the door and heard nothing from within.

He kicked in the door.

Fin sprang up, grabbed his weapons, and guarded the opening. The band could not enter. When they thrust their spears in, Fin sliced off the spearheads. Several members of the attacking force climbed up onto the roof of the hut and tore off the thatch. Then Wulfgar, mustering every ounce of strength he had, rose up onto his feet, grabbed a spear, and thrust it up impaling the men who were attempting to descend on him.

The effort expended in his attack was more than his weakened body could stand, and Wulfgar the Stalwart toppled down onto the floor in a heap. When Fin heard his brother's fall, he was distracted and Hook bounded into the hut.

Hook ran his sword through Fin's heart. He stepped over the lad's body and approached the sprawled form of the stalwart.

With an Anglo-Saxon war cry he swooped his sword down through the massive neck of the outlaw, held the severed head aloft and roared the laugh of the victor.

It is said that when the sheep that still grazed on the plateau became aware of the death of the three men with whom they had lived were dead, that Wulfgar's and Fin's sweet-ewes mourned. The same could not be said for Unferth's lover.

Lord Wyrd sat on his throne at the root of Yggdrasil, the Universe Ash Tree. The wyrd he had dictated to his daughters at Wulfgar's birth had been spun out, allowing the ghost of a stalwart outlaw to wend its way into the spirit-world of Hel.

It is not given to any mortal to know what happens to a mortal spirit once it enters that Underworld Kingdom.

Only the gods of Valhalla can follow the further adventures of Wulfgar the Stalwart's adventures in the Kingdom of Hel.

Those Friggin' Horny Anglo-Saxon Gods

Chapter One.
GOODBYE BALLS

The race of Gnomes dwells in mines and caves beneath the earth's surface.

These small creatures are industrious miners and smiths who create beautiful works of art and fabulous jewelry from the gold, silver and precious stones they extract from the earth's depths.

They are small, amphibious, ugly, horny, and mean little sons of guns.

Not that they see themselves as ugly. To them small, hunchbacked, hairy creatures whose toenails grow out at the rate of two inches a day are perceived as handsome and charming.

They are a very promiscuous race.

But, as with any group of creatures, some are hornier than others.

The brothers Alvis and Mim surpassed their fellow Gnomes in lasciviousness.

And Alvis was even more randy than Mim.

One day, Alvis was so hard up for ass he could barely contain himself.

So, as happened with fair regularity, he scooted up the mine shaft to the upper world in search of sexual adventure.

The only implement he carried up with him was his pair of silver scissors.

He never went anywhere without them.

Without his regular pedicure, his damned toenails became downright unwieldy.

Alvis had heard that the Wæterelfen who lived in the Sea of Wyrd (Sea of *Fate*) were hot numbers.

Being amphibious, he could live beneath the surface of the sea and hopefully could get some sweet loving from the Wæterelfen.

The Wæterelfen were the daughters of the Lord of Wyrd (the master of fate, whose daughters were the Norns and the Wæterelfen).

The Wæterelfen were three gorgeous creatures of lesbian persuasion who were inclined to be somewhat stupid.

And although they did not favor males as sex partners, they were notorious teases.

The Lord of Wyrd had stashed a cache of magic gold in his sea. And, not realizing what a bunch of ditzes his daughters were, he suffered them to guard the hoard.

Alvis, in his poontang search, reached the shores of the mighty sea and slithered beneath the surface. He descended to the bottom and looked around to see if he could spot any of the hot Wæterelfen sisters.

As far as he knew, the sisters could be swimming around anywhere within the sea.

He settled down for a while in hopes that one or two, or three might come swimming by.

While he was waiting, he clipped his toenails to make himself as attractive as possible to the babes.

When he put the scissors away, his urgent erection began to drive him nuts.

When no action appeared, he decided he might as well engage in a bit of self abuse and relieve the erotic pressure.

Thus, the Gnome was so engaged with his prick that he did not notice that the three Wæterelfen had swum into the area and were frolicking three cubits above his bent head.

The sisters, at first, were incognizant of the little creature bent over on the river's bottom.

They didn't notice him because they were too busy playing their everlasting games with each other's bodies.

Smoothly swimming around each other, they rubbed bodies, sucked nipples, gobbled at crotches, and maneuvered through the hundred thousand sex games possible for creatures who are equally comfortable underwater and on land.

Caught up in their constant orgy, the three were hardly competent guards of their father's magical golden hoard.

One of the sexy creatures, Beyla by name, spied the ugly gnome down below playing with himself.

"Yo-ho, Sisters," she cried. "Take a gander down below. It's time to change sports. Let's see if we can drive the little bastard nuts with a bit of teasing.

"Let's get down there fast, before he climaxes, so he'll be hot to trot, and we'll keep him from getting a chance to release his load."

Vestri swam down behind the gnome and tapped him gently on the back.

Alvis jumped up and spun around.

Beyla easily swam away from him. Nidi swam up behind him and ran a finger up his rectum, giving a rub to his prostate.

When he spun around again to see what was up, she was out of his range. But Vestri was now behind him again.

She reached between his legs and grabbed his balls.

The three continued their teasing sex play.

Alvis found a slender, lovely hand running up his staff. Then felt a pair of breasts slithering up his back.

He was having the time of his life.

But he was getting desperate.

It was one thing to have the three lovely creatures teasing him.

But he had left Gnomeland in search of poontang.

All he needed was to catch hold of one of those ditzes and he'd have his ready hardon in her before she knew it.

He kept trying to catch a nymph, only always to find out she could out-maneuver him.

The Gnome's balls began to ache in his desperation.

And as he was beginning to feel very sorry for himself, the sun rose.

Its rays penetrated to the bottom of the sea.

Alvis shaded his eyes and looked up to get a sharper view of the wily Wæterelfen.

As he looked, he saw that the sun's rays had illuminated something that gleamed brighter than gold.

Like all Gnomes, Alvis thought he knew everything there was to know about gold. But what he was looking at had a strange, mystical glimmer unlike any metal he had ever dealt with before.

"What is that I'm looking at?" he asked the lovelies.

"Oh," Nidi told him. "That's daddy's gold. We're here to guard it."

"Guard it?" Alvis thought to himself. "You ditzes do one hell of a job guarding it. All you think about is screwing around playing your stoop tag with each other and teasing any male who comes your way."

But, instead of mouthing the sarcasm, he took a soft approach to attempt to find out about that gleaming gold.

"Your daddy's gold, eh? And just who *is* your father?"

"The Lord of Wyrd, of course, Shorty," Vestri laughed. "He owns the magic gold that everyone in the world covets. So he hid it right here in this sea. And no one knows where it is but us."

"You three certainly are wonderful guardians of your father's magical gold," the crafty gnome complemented. "Just what is it that makes it magical? Is it simply that it glimmers brighter than other gold?"

"Oh, no, Stupid," Beyla scoffed. "What makes it special is that if anyone should get a piece of it and fashion a ring, he would become Master of the Age. That person would, or could, be able to amass vast riches and control other people."

The greedy little gnome forgot all about why he was there. He had left Gnomeland to seek sex.

Power, though. Now *there* was something really worthwhile to pursue.

All concern about his aching balls evaporated.

"That is very interesting," Alvis said. "And you three are such wonderful guards.

"You say that all a thief would have to do is abscond with enough of that gold to make a ring. And then he would be Master of the Age.

"Isn't there more to it than that?"

"Well," Nidi had to admit. "There is that one little hitch. Which is why it's so easy for us to guard the Wyrdgold. Because no man would ever want to do what it takes to forge a ring from it."

'Oh?" Alvis wondered. "Why would that be?"

"Because of the catch, Dummy," she responded. "I already told you that."

"And what's the catch?" the Gnome pressed.

"Oh, that," the water nymph scoffed. "The thief would have to cut off his balls and leave them here with the rest of the gold. Otherwise the ring would be nothing special at all.

"We know that no man would cut off his balls and renounce sex, no matter what the prize."

"You're right, of course," the avaricious gnome answered, knowing he would willingly renounce sex for power. "You have nothing to worry about there."

As Alvis was talking to the three scatterbrains, he was edging himself toward the golden cache.

He set his mighty little legs into a springing set and leaped right onto the pile of Wyrdgold.

He whipped out his silver shears, cut off his balls with one snip, dropped them onto the pile, grabbed a chunk of gold, and launched himself out onto the shore.

As he hastened away from the sea, ball-less but elated, the miraculous gold chunk in hand, he laughed uproariously, heading back to Gnomeland.

The sound of the sobbing Wæterelfen, sitting on an island in their sea, only served to heighten Alvis's pleasure.

Chapter Two.
HAIL VALHALLA

The same dawn that revealed the Wyrdgold to Alvis awakened Woden, the king of the gods.

He awoke with an erection, as usual.

He nudged his wife, Frida, in order to awaken her to a new day.

"Wake up, Frida. What I want is some loving."

"You wake me up to tell me you want to make love?" Frida replied angrily. "You think that's news? You always want to do it.

"You wake me up every morning wanting to do the same thing. So we hump before breakfast. Then, after breakfast you go up to the roof to talk to your damned crow, Munin."

"He's not a crow, damn it," Woden corrected. "He's a raven."

"Crow, raven, what's the difference?" the queen of the gods growled.

"What he is is your pander. He's always flying around to find some mortal bitch in heat so you can sneak out of here to be unfaithful to me."

Woden had stopped listening about halfway through his wife's rant and was applying his lips to Frida's nipples.

Frida was beautifully endowed in the breast department. And had nipples to die for.

She cut short her harangue. She was getting moist in the cunt department and spread her legs for the pre-breakfast romp she had to admit she really enjoyed even more than bitching at her husband.

When they had each climaxed a few times (what's the use of being a god if you can't have multiple orgasms?) Woden began to get dressed.

"Woden," Frida scolded. "Put on your gods damned eyepatch. You cannot leave this bedroom without it in place.

"When gods and mortals see your empty eye-socket it makes them gag. King of gods or not, you've got to remember the patch."

Woden reminded his wife that he had given his left eye as the price to get a drink from the Norn's Well of Wisdom.

"You sure got a royal screwing on *that* one," Frida told him, not for the first time.

"Talk about getting gypped. Since you had that 'wisdom sip' you've done a real lot of truly stupid things…" she continued.

She was ready to go on with her spiel.

Woden cut her off with, "Yes, dear. I'll put on the gods damned eye patch."

Peace reigned in the bedroom long enough for the couple to go to the window to see how work was proceeding on Valhalla, the new castle Woden was having built across the gully from their bedroom.

Woden had hired two brothers, giants, Ægir and Vanir, to build Valhalla for him and his fellow gods and goddesses.

The day was starting out great. The couple could see that the castle was really completed at last.

"I suppose the boys will be coming by to collect their pay, now that the job is done," Frida sighed.

The matter of the contract Woden had made with the two builders was a continual source of discord between the god and the goddess.

With the able assistance of Loki, the god of fire, mischief, and deceit, Woden had struck a deal with Ægir and Vanir that when they completed building Valhalla, they could have his sister-in-law Freya, the goddess of love, fertility, and sexual pleasure, to enjoy at will. Not just once, mind you. But forever.

"What a stupid contract *that* was," Frida criticized. "Just like a male. That is *my* sister you're giving them for your damned castle.

"I hated the castle idea before the first stone was laid. And now that it's finished, I still hate it even more.

"And you know what I hate most about it?"

Woden knew but also knew he couldn't stop his wife's rant.

"It's that secret door you insisted on, so you can get out and away from me and chase all the women and goddesses that crow of yours…"

"Raven!" Woden insisted.

Thinking of the women he hoped Munin had lined up for him for the day gave the god a brand new erection.

But he had to forget it for now and get his wife quieted down.

"If I've told you once, I've told you a thousand times," Woden explained. "I'm not about to give Freya to the big stoops.

"I'd always planned to stiff the giant dummies."

"But they made you inscribe your contract with them in runes on your sacred spear," Frida pointed out.

"I know, I know," Woden explained. "But when Loki was helping me make the deal, he said he'd come up with something sneaky when it came time to pay the boys for the job."

Munin landed on the window sill.

"Psst, Boss," the bird told Woden. "Red alert. Your sister-in-law Freya's on her way here now. And those two big boobs, Vanir and Ægir, aren't far behind her."

The news turned out to be a bit late.

Because Freya burst into the bedroom just at that moment.

Frida had slipped on a robe. But the only thing Woden had on was his eyepatch.

The king and queen continued dressing themselves even as Freya was yapping.

"Oh, Frida," she addressed her sister.

"Did you see? The damned castle's completed.

"And those big louts who built it are on their way right now to collect...me."

Woden told his sister-in-law to cool it.

"Cut the crap!" he ordered.

"It was Loki's idea to trade you for the castle. And he guaranteed me that he'd think up some way to get us out of giving you to the two jerks when the time came."

"Loki!" Freya scoffed. "He's the biggest screw-up of all us gods. The god of fire, ha! I don't trust him."

"And neither do I," Frida answered. "And I never did."

As the rather unpleasant conversation was progressing, who should come busting into the royal bedroom but Vanir and Ægir, the two man construction company.

The royal couple had finished getting dressed while holding the rather one-sided discussion with Freya. So they met the giant builders with some semblance of dignity.

The boys wanted Freya. She was such a hot babe. And now, thinking they were about to get their paws on her after all the sweaty labor they had expended on building Valhalla, their giant dongs were apparent to the divine family gathering.

To their demand for the babe, Woden laughed.

"Ha, ha, Boys. I'm sorry, but I just cannot give Freya to you. When we made our little contract, I was only kidding. What would you like instead of my sister-in-law?"

It was clear the giants were not amused by Woden's little joke.

Woden had a very real reason that he never intended to give Frida's sister to the ungainly giants. And the reason was not what you might think.

Freya was the apple girl. She was the goddess of youth and sexual passion.

She had a garden she guarded. No other god or goddess had jurisdiction over that apple patch of hers.

Without a golden apple a day, the gods and goddesses would lose their mojo.

Goodbye hardons. Farewell moist, welcoming koozies.

There was no way Woden would let that happen.

Where was that damned Loki? He was supposed to be there when the crisis arrived. He had promised to come up with something at the right time.

As the girls had just recently said, "What a screw-up!"

Vanir and Ægir were not going to take this bullshit sitting down.

They were big and strong.

They decided between the two of them to just grab the bitch and haul her away.

Or, perhaps, just take her right there in that bedroom to get the ball rolling.

Before they could act, though, Freya's two brothers, Thor, the god of thunder and battles, and Tugh, the god of war and warriors, came busting in.

Somehow they apparently had gotten word of what was happening.

Thor flourished his constant weapon, his hammer, at the giants.

Tugh clenched his fists, ready to take on whoever brother Thor was not about to accost.

Woden got his spear from the corner where he had left it the previous night and stepped between the combatants.

"Now, now, Boys," he commanded. "There'll be no fighting here. "Loki will be arriving soon and will work this business out in a jiffy."

And, what do you know. The god of mischief and deceit did, indeed, come sliding into the room, right on cue.

He was full of big news, and insisted on telling his story before the others in the room could get in a word edgewise.

"Guess where I've just been?" he asked, without waiting for an answer.

"I just got back from the Wyrdan Sea. You know. Where those dumb broads, the Wæterelfen, do their thing?

"Well, maybe you know, and maybe you don't, but Lord Wyrd has a hoard of magic gold. And he has it stashed away in his sea.

"And all his ditzy blonde daughters have to do is guard the treasure.

"Now, you might ask, what is all so magic about that gold?

"Well, I'll tell you what's so magic about that stash of gold.

"If anyone can get to it and make off with a chunk, guess what? All he has to do is forge a ring out of it. And the wearer of that ring becomes Master of the Age.

"Yes, sir. Master of the Age. All the riches and sex are his for the asking. Except that he has to cut off his balls and leave them in the sea to be able to forge the ring.

"And guess what I just received as hot news from the Wæterelfen?

"They screwed up royally. While they were playing stoop-tag with each other, that wretched Gnome, Alvis, made off with a chunk of the magic gold. And he left his balls behind so he could craft the magic ring.

"He headed back to Gnomeland. He and his brother Mim are master craftsmen, as you know. And probably they have already crafted the gods damned ring!"

Talk about a show stopper!

Everyone present suddenly wanted that ring.

The possessor of the magic ring would no longer need Freya's golden apples. The ring would supply the owner with eternal mojo.

To say nothing of control over everyone and everything that exists in the Age.

And unlimited wealth and riches.

The giants would much rather have the ring than Freya.

Frida, in turn, wanted the ring to be able to control her husband's philandering. If she had that ring, Woden would have to get his sexual jollies only at home.

And, of course, Woden wanted the ring himself for the raw power and the unlimited sex it would afford him.

Everyone present was content to put the matter of the payment for Valhalla on hold until sunset. The giants agreed not to fuck Freya until then. And if the ransom was available to them at that time, Woden, Frida, Thor, and Tugh could have their family member back.

Otherwise she would be the giants' plaything to enjoy forevermore.

So Woden and Loki headed out of there and set out for the mine shaft to Gnomeland.

They were determined to steal the ring from that despicable little jerk, Alvis.

After that, they would deal with the two dummies who were holding Freya hostage.

Chapter Three.
A VISIT TO GNOMELAND

Before Woden and Loki could get to Gnomeland, Alvis and his brother Mim had already worked the Wyrdgold into two artifacts.

First, and most important, of course, was the ring.

Even though his brother Mim was a more skilled craftsman, Alvis had to forge the ring himself. He was the one who had sacrificed his balls.

And with the remaining gold, Mim crafted the much more delicate job of fashioning a remarkable helmet, the Tarn helmet, which rendered the wearer either invisible or into a shape shifter.

Because Alvis was very avaricious, the first task he set for the magic ring he now wore was to force all the Gnomes in Gnomeland to bring piles of the wealth of their kingdom into his own cave.

By the time Woden and Loki arrived, there was an enormous pile of beautiful artifacts fashioned of gold, silver, and precious jewels sitting in Alvis' cave.

As the two gods stepped into his chamber, Alvis was rubbing his hands together and gloating over the wealth that was now exclusively his.

He was actually happy to see Woden and Loki enter. Here were two gods he felt he was now truly superior to.

He loved to be able to brag to these beings who had always before been his superiors.

He picked up his Tarn helmet and greeted them with a welcoming bow.

"So, ho," he said. "Now that I am Master of the Age, even the haughty Woden and the sly Loki deign to visit me."

Loki responded.

"Yes, Alvis. We are now very awed by your power. And, I might add, by your wealth.

"Woden. Would you look at that pile of treasure stashed up in this cave? Have you ever seen such a valuable cache?"

"A beautiful treasure trove," Woden concurred, playing into whatever scam Loki was perpetrating.

"And that golden helmet, Alvis," Loki continued. "How exquisitely made. I must congratulate you."

"Pooh," Alvis scoffed, not admitting that his brother had made it.

"Everything we Gnomes create at our forges is a marvel. But this particular helmet I have in hand has very special qualities. It is wrought of magical gold."

"Fabulous!" Loki exclaimed. "You are a wonder, Alvis. Just what are those special qualities?"

Alvis was having the time of his life being able to brag to the two gods about how clever he was.

"When I wear this helmet, I can choose for it to perform either of two functions for me. I can have it make me invisible. Or it can allow me to shift shapes."

"Oh, *do* demonstrate for us," Loki encouraged.

"Isn't he clever, though, Woden?"

"Astoundingly so," Woden played along.

"Just watch," Alvis said, placing the Tarn helmet on his head.

True to one of its properties, it rendered the Gnome invisible.

He ran, unseen, behind Woden and slapped the king of the gods on the ass.

Woden was not amused. He rose to his full dignified height and smiled contemptuously.

Alvis sneaked up to Loki and gave him a playful goose up his arse. Loki feigned amusement.

And knowing exactly where the loathsome Gnome had to be to give him the goose, Loki reached back and grabbed him exactly where he knew his balls would have to be.

Of course, there were no balls there, which was still somewhat embarrassing to the gnome. And really annoyed little Alvis.

It ruined his fun.

He stamped his foot in pique and removed the helmet.

"That wasn't nice," Alvis complained.

"Sorry," Loki said contritely.

"Now, what is this shape shifting trick you can do?" Loki asked with a malicious grin.

"I can change myself into any kind of creature I want when I'm wearing my magic helmet," Alvis blustered.

"Any shape?" Loki questioned with a doubtful smirk.

"Any shape," Alvis confirmed.

"Even something as difficult as becoming a toad?" Loki asked scoffingly.

"Becoming a toad would be a cinch," Alvis proclaimed.

"I somehow have to doubt that," Loki led the Gnome on.

"Oh, yeah?" Alvis scoffed. "Just you watch, Smartypants."

He put on the helmet and changed immediately into a toad.

Woden rapidly stepped on the little critter.

Loki grabbed its head, removing the helmet, and Alvis became his gnomish self again.

Immediately, Woden grabbed the helmet away from Alvis's reach.

Loki instantly snatched the ring off Alvis's finger and handed it to Woden.

The gods tied Alvis up.

Woden placed the ring on his own finger and ordered all the Gnomes in Gnomeland to haul the treasure from Alvis' cave up to the earth's surface.

The Gnomes of course obeyed, and, in a long line, bore the great treasure pile up the shaft and onto the earth's surface.

The two gods followed the string of Gnomes into the shaft.

And as they set foot at the chamber door, Alvis shouted a curse at the ring, proclaiming in his malediction that it would ultimately do no more for its future owners than it had done for him.

Woden exited the cave first.

Loki followed, laughing at the wretched Gnome who had presumed to become Master of the Age and whose curse was now attached to the ring.

Chapter Four.
THE RANSOM

When Woden and Loki got out of the shaft and onto the earth's surface, the Gnomes were standing around the precious hoard.

Woden ordered them to take the treasure to the field just outside the old palace, where Frida was nervously awaiting her husband and Loki.

It was the hour before sundown, and brothers Thor and Tugh had been watching the gold, silver, and jewels arrive, borne by an army of Gnomes.

The boys had hurried to the field, relieved that a ransom had obviously been secured for their sister Freya.

Woden and Loki arrived at the site just in time to see the giants arriving with Freya held between them.

Woden stepped up to the giants, pointed to the piled up treasure, and addressed them.

"Well, well, Vanir and Ægir. Here we are before sundown as agreed. You see that accumulation of treasure over there. It exceeds the wealth even of all us gods.

"We offer it to you as ransom for Freya.

"With all that worth, you can buy enough willing lascivious and eager women to keep yourselves erotically engaged from now to the end of the Age."

Woden was quite pleased with his pretty speech.

Vanir answered the king of the gods.

"My brother and I entered into the building project which, as you can see, right across that gully, is completed and on schedule.

"We had our hearts set on getting Freya in exchange for all our hard work. That's what you promised. And the contract is spelled out in runes on that very spear you're carrying.

"You and Loki now are trying to back out of a legal contract.

"All right. We still want Freya. But we're willing to negotiate. Aren't we Ægir?"

Ægir grunted a "yes."

"So," Vanir continued. "You're offering us that pile of junk over there instead of Freya. We don't know what it's really worth.

"But tell you what we're willing to do.

"You pile up all those goodies, and build a wall out of it around this goddess we've got between us here. We'll accept the booty as payment if the stuff's piled up high enough and tight enough so none of us can see Freya behind it. Once she's totally surrounded by the treasure, we'll haul the junk away and we'll call it a deal."

Loki thought that Woden should haggle a bit. But Woden knew Frida, Freya, Tugh, and Thor wouldn't stand for that.

And, besides, with the ring he'd be ahead on the deal anyway.

Everyone except the giants and Freya got busy building a wall around the love goddess.

What a glitter of precious metals, artifacts, and jewels graced the rays of the setting sun.

"There," Loki exclaimed to the giants at long last when every bit of the hoard had been piled up around the goddess of the golden apples. "The golden wall surrounds and hides Freya. We'll just tear down a section to free her, and the loot is yours and Freya will be back among us."

"Not so fast there, Chum," Vanir warned. "Freya is still visible behind that wall. A deal's a deal. The wall has to hide her completely. I can still see parts of her through some chinks. Can't you, Ægir?"

Ægir grunted his agreement and pointed out that he could clearly see Freya's left nipple and her twat through two chinks in the constructed wall.

There was no argument against the observation. Everyone had to agree that the goddess' left nipple and her hot twat were still visible through two chinks in the wall of treasure.

Loki was clinging tight to the Tarn helmet.

Vanir insisted, "That gold thing you've got there, Loki. That should just about conceal Freya's left boob."

Everyone present agreed with Vanir, and Loki reluctantly gave up the treasured item.

Vanir closed the chink with the Tarn helmet and nodded his satisfaction.

He then pointed to the ring that Woden had unsuccessfully attempted to keep hidden.

"That gold thing there," the giant insisted. "Give it to me and let's see if it'll cover that glimpse I still have of her twat that we can all still see through that chink in the wall of junk."

Woden knew he'd lost the game. He couldn't renege at this point.

He handed the magic ring to Vanir.

The ring that gave its possessor mastery of the Age closed the chink.
The ransom was paid.
The giants dismantled the wall.
Freya stepped out into the arms of her sister and her two brothers.

The deal was done.

Vanir immediately began throwing the treasure into a big bag he'd brought for the purpose.
Ægir hurried over to get some of the loot for himself.
He reached down to grab the ring.
As he leaned over, Vanir raised his enormous club and struck his brother dead.
He put on the helmet and turned invisible.
Vanir stalked off, wearing the ring and the Tarn helmet, and dragging his loot in his great tote-bag.
So all that the observers could see was an enormous bag full of unimaginable treasure apparently bearing itself away into the setting sun.
And the corpse of the giant, Ægir, lay bleeding into the rich earth of the field unheeded by the departing Vanir.

Woden and Loki were desolate over the loss of the ring and the helmet.
Frida, Freya, and their two brothers were jubilant over Freya's release.

Frida looked across the gully at the castle that had been the cause of the whole crisis.
"Look, Woden," she called out. "There's Valhalla, the castle you just bought.
"And there's a rainbow bridge extending to it from here. Let's go over and check out what you've paid for."
Woden lamented that he had paid very dearly indeed for his new castle.

But arm in arm, the king and queen of the gods led the rest of the gods and goddesses across the rainbow and into their new home, Valhalla.

Chapter Five.
WODEN'S BROOD

Vanir, the possessor of the ring, the helmet and the treasure hoard, had stomped off to the East Forest.

He and his brother had labored hard to build the blooming castle for the gods.

Vanir was naturally lazy, and was pooped from the job he'd done, and from the mental gymnastics he'd had to exercise to get all that loot from Woden and Loki.

All he wanted to do now was sleep.

When he arrived at a clearing in the East Forest, he found a nice, comfortable cave.

He put on the shape-shifting Tarn helmet and changed himself into an enormous, ferocious, venom fanged dragon.

He piled up his treasure on the floor of the cave, placed the ring atop the hoard, lay down atop his belongings, and settled down into a nice satisfying snooze.

He planned to stay in his cave, guarding his treasure, day and night forever. He would emerge only once a day, at high noon, to get a drink of water from a near-by pool and to take a piss.

And, when luck provided, he could, at the same time, gobble up anyone who might happen along within easy reach.

While Vanir slept, life went on at Valhalla.

Thanks to Freya's golden apples, Woden suffered no problems with erectile dysfunction. And his raven, Munin, kept him well supplied with willing, even exuberant, lovelies.

Once informed of where a hot number was waiting, Woden was out the secret door and away from Frieda's purview in a trice.

Our story now skips ahead some twenty years or so.

During the twenty year hiatus, Woden had made godlike love to every chick who turned him on.

Many were one-night stands, of course.

So many women. And hopefully an Age to savor them in.

But Woden also had a few long-term affairs.

One of those affairs was with Yortha, the Great Earth Mother.

That affair lasted for ten years. A much longer relationship than was Woden's wont.

Yortha was, and is, enormous. She had and has the largest breasts in the universe. If Woden weren't a god, he could have gotten himself suffocated between those hooters.

And she has a vagina you could drive a caravan of horses through. A mortal could get lost up that canal.

But since both Woden and Yortha were gods, they easily managed to make the necessary adjustments to fit their parts snuggly together.

Over the course of the affair, Yortha bore nine daughters who were known as the Valkyries. The youngest of whom, who was clearly Woden's favorite, was named Brynhildr.

These sturdy Valkyries were given the job of scavenging battlefields for fallen heroes who were whisked up to Valhalla to serve as castle guards.

But more of that later.

Another female playmate that Munin found for Woden was a little sweetie named Yrsa.

That relationship produced a pair of twins, a boy named Sigmond and a girl named Signy.

Those kids formed part of a secret plan Woden had hatched, with Loki's advice, to get back the ring that Vanir had carried away.

Woden couldn't go get the ring back himself. After all, he had given it to Vanir to get Freya and her aphrodisiac apples back. He needed his daily apple to keep his mojo flowing.

And he was absolutely bound to the contract that was engraved in runes on his sacred spear.

Woden's secret plan, if you want to know, was that when the twins grew up, they were supposed to fall in love, make love, and produce a hero, to be named Sigord. Then it would be Sigord's job to wrest the ring and the helmet away from Vanir.

Once his grandson Sigord managed to get the ring and helmet back from the giant, he was expected to give them back to good old Grand-dad. Who, as planned by Loki, would have gotten the prizes back by guile without having abrogated the sacred contract.

It was a pretty complicated deal. Perhaps a bit shady. And certainly crafty. Yet, legal within the letter of the laws that govern gods and men.

Woden lived with Yrsa and his little family for twelve years under the name of Wulf.

The twins, of mixed race, god and mortal, were called Volsongs.

When Signy was only five, she was abducted from the family by a nefarious blackguard named Hagbard, while she was playing unattended outside the family hut.

Hagbard took her off to his own hut, which had been constructed around an ash tree.

And he forced Signy to marry him.

Signy was an unhappy child bride.

Woden hung around the family hut with his family of Yrsa and Sigmond for another seven years after Signy's abduction.

He taught his son, Sigmond, how to use a sword and a spear. He took him out hunting and camping in the forest. He let Sigmond know that he expected great things of him.

And, very importantly, he advised him that sometime in the future, when the lad would find himself in deep doodoo, he would find a dandy sword in an unexpected place.

He drilled that information into the kid's thick skull lest he forget.

Little Sigmond was strong as an ox.

But, unfortunately, he was not too awfully bright.

After a few years, Woden got tired of being tied down in his little domestic arrangement with Yrsa and the kid.

So he told his earthly family he was off to the wars.

And he never returned.

When Sigmond turned eighteen, he bade his mother goodbye and left home to join the army.

In his very first battle his side lost.

And the sword he had with him got shattered.

Sigmond did not worry too much about the loss of the sword. It had been beaten into his head well enough by Daddy that if he was really ever desperately in need of a sword, it would become available in some unexpected place.

Since Sigmond's side had lost the battle, and perhaps had even lost whatever war they were waging, Sigmond saw no need to hang around the battlefield.

And besides, the weather had turned rather nasty and he was getting sopping wet.

So he wandered off into the forest seeking shelter of any kind.

He roamed around for quite a while before he found a rude hovel built around a huge ash tree.

He didn't bother to knock on the door. He was not particularly known for his good manners. He just broke in and fell on the floor exhausted.

Inside the hut, his long-lost twin sister, Signy, was startled by the sudden entrance and collapse of the young man.

Sigmond managed to gasp, "Water."

Signy brought a horn of water to where Sigmond's prostrate form was spread out on the floor.

Cradling his head with one hand, she brought the horn to his mouth.

Being a hardy soul, the water revived Sigmond sufficiently that, with the nice young lady's assistance, he was able to stand and stagger to one of the chairs at the rough-hewn table.

The two sat at the table and stared at each other.

They very much liked what they saw.

Signy asked the handsome stranger what had brought him to her hut.

He told her about the lost battle and his retreat due to his broken sword.

"Are you wounded?" she asked.

Seeing a chance to take advantage of the situation, Sigmond replied, "I'm not sure. If you could help me off with my clothes, we could check."

Signy had fallen hard for the gorgeous, muscular stranger.

She agreed to help him out of his clothing so she could check his wounds.

They were both happy to discover that the hero had no wounds.

And they were happier yet that he was now naked.

In order that her guest not feel embarrassed by his nakedness while she was clothed, Signy disrobed as well.

It seemed like a good time to offer her guest a welcoming horn of mead.

They each took deep swigs of the liquor.

Signy fingered the horn suggestively.

Sigmond got the picture.

"What's your name?" she asked.

"Woebegone," he answered, indicating that he'd had a tough time of it up 'til then.

"What's yours?"

"That name would fit me, too," Signy answered, indicating that life had been no bed of roses for her either.

They each took another swig from the horn and looked deeply into each other's eyes. Then they ran their hands over each other's body.

Signy sighed, panted, and whispered, "My husband's name is Hagbard and he's hunting."

"Hagbard is hunting?" Sigmond questioned.

"Yes," she reiterated. "Hagbard is hunting and probably won't be back home for a while."

"When husband Hagbard gets back from hunting, do you think he might be a little put out to find us here messing around?" Sigmond asked archly.

Signy told him that was a very real possibility.

Since Sigmond was swordless, he felt that on hubby's return he might find himself in deep doodoo.

When he pointed out his dilemma to the nifty babe, she mentioned to him that there was a sword embedded in the trunk of the ash tree that stood smack dab in the middle of the hut.

She let him know that the sword had been thrust into the tree trunk by a one-eyed stranger many years before.

The stranger had told Hagbard and her that only a true hero could ever pull the sword out of the tree trunk.

Many had attempted the feat. None had succeeded.

"But," Signy assured him. "I happen to have a sheath right here. Would you care to see if you can get your weapon into it before Hubby gets home?"

Sigmond, a very responsive hero, showed himself ready on the spot.

"That weapon looks pretty good to me" Signy told him.

"Then let's do what comes naturally," the hero suggested.

And before you knew it the twins were at it like a couple of martens.

There was the sound of hoofbeats outside, followed by a whinny. The master of the hut was returning from his hunting trip.

The merry couple broke off their happy engagement in a hurry, got back into their clothing, and were sitting politely at the table as the master of the hut entered.

Now there is nothing in the world that looks more like a couple that has just been playing the two-backed beast than a couple that has just been playing the two-backed beast.

Nor is there a scent that smells more like that of a couple that has just been engaged in hanky-panky than that of a couple that has just been engaged in hanky-panky.

When Hagbard stepped into the hut, he saw his wife sitting at the table with a young stud.

The couple's clothes were in disarray.

The dissimilating looks on the couple's faces were tell-tale. And the scent of recent coupling was redolent in the air.

There was no doubt in the man's mind that his wife had been messing around big time with her husky table companion.

Hagbard gave Signy a questioning look.

She could not control a blush.

Hagbard knew that he would have to kill the stranger who had come to his home and had been messing around with his wife.

The various tribes that dwelt in the forests were governed by different laws.

But one law was shared by all. The law of hospitality.

Hagbard, like all men everywhere, was bound by that law.

He would have to feed the stranger and would be obliged to allow him to stay overnight safely in the hut.

But, at dawn the next morning, Hagbard would have discharged his obligation and would be free to exercise the right of every husband.

He had to kill the man who had dishonored him.

Hagbard did not greet his guest. He knew he could not control his anger yet.

Sigmond knew better than to address his host. Menace hung over the encounter. It was best to hold one's peace.

"Food," Hagbard grunted at his wife.

He plunked himself down at the table, staring balefully at his guest.

Signy arose, went to the stove, ladled the bubbling stew into bowls and silently set the bowls on the table.

She poured water into three goblets, set them on the table, and wordlessly took her place between the two men.

Hagbard stared at his bowl and then at his wife and the stranger.

He noted that the two shared nearly identical physiognomy. Yes, the stranger's face was clearly of masculine cast while his wife's was decidedly feminine.

Oh, yes. One had breasts which the other did not. However that other one had a penis that was outlined behind the tight-fitting pants. And, hmmm. The one with the breasts had a twat that, as her husband, he was well aware of.. But she did not have the musculature of the other.

But other than those notable differences, it would be difficult to tell one from the other.

Well…other than the beard on the jerk who had come visiting uninvited.

Curious.

Hagbard lifted his bowl to his lips and slurped.

The guilty appearing couple followed suit.

The glances that passed between his wife and the intruder confirmed what Hagbard had sensed from the outset. There'd been some screwing around in the hut all right.

Hagbard set down his bowl and was in control of himself enough to speak.

Glaring at Sigmond he asked, "Who the Hell are you?"

"My name is Woebegone, son of Wulf."

"More!" Hagbard demanded, apparently giving up any interest in his meal.

"I was born in the North Forest," the guest replied. "My sister was abducted by a tribe of scoundrels when I was five. I was raised by a warrior named Wulf who deserted my mother and me when I was twelve. I have had a hard life since then, so I go by the name of Woebegone."

Hagbard did the math. He recalled the raid his tribe had made in the North Forest eighteen years previously. A girl who was about five years old at the time had been left playing by herself outside a hut.

He had taken the child and brought her to his hut in the East Forest and had married her there.

Hagbard addressed Woebegone.

"Me, Scoundrel. You, Bad News. Tonight, you sleep here. Tomorrow, we meet outside hut. Fight. I kill you."

Sigmond figured that about wrapped up the conversation.

His host would meet him for manly battle in the morning.

His host clearly had both a sword and a spear.

He, himself, had no weapon whatsoever. His broken sword had been left behind on the battlefield.

Sigmond had a potential problem on his hands.

Hagbard had said everything he needed to say to his overnight guest.

He addressed his wife.

"Time for bed," he announced. "Go fix night-time drink and bring to bedroom."

And with that he stomped off into the boudoir.

Hagbard was accustomed to having an evening toddy before retiring. It was a concoction wife Signy knew how to prepare to perfection.

Once hubby had closed the bedroom door behind him, Signy got down the drinking horn and poured the mead and honeywater mix into it.

She winked at her new boyfriend.

She went to the pantry and brought out a sleeping potion which she added to the brew.

Sigmond caught the import immediately.

Then the lass pointed to the sword embedded in the ash tree and winked again.

Communication between the couple was complete as Signy disappeared into the bedroom with the mickey she had prepared for her loving husband.

Sigmond waited for what seemed an eternity before his newfound love came back into the room with a smile that said to him "Do me again."

Sigmond knew for sure that his host was dozing in a deep sleep in the next room.

Sigmond was not a novice at making love. The North Forest had a few scattered settlements. Although he was not a member of any of the tribes in the area, none of them was hostile to him and his father Wulf.

He had encountered many willing maidens in the forest who had happily provided him with a handy supply of carnal knowledge.

Signy shed her garments, displaying a pair of knockers that were a nifty eyeful.

Sigmond took her in his arms, lowered his lips to her nipples and cupped her crotch with exploring hands.

How stimulating were her perky nipples. How moist and inviting her cunt.

He lifted her and set her gently on the dirt floor.

He prepared to mount her when she indicated she wanted him to lie on his back first.

Previously, when they had fucked prior to Hagbard's return, they had plunged right into the act.

Now Signy wanted to explore the physique of her lover.

To Sigmond, this was indeed a novelty.

The girls he had met in the forest back in the North Forest had been his to meet, fuck and forget.

This one wanted to make love to his body.

In return, he felt her up as well.

And with the husband asleep in the next room, how satisfying it was when he made sweet love to this honey.

It was a moment unlike anything either of them had previously experienced.

When their lovemaking culminated in a glorious climax, they relaxed into considering what the morrow was likely to bring.

They stared at the sword that was ensconced in the tree trunk that dominated the room.

Sigmond nodded towards the weapon, indicating a desire to know what it was all about.

Signy told him about the one-eyed stranger who had dropped by some years previously holding a spear in one hand and the sword in the other.

One-eyed stranger? Daddy perhaps?

Signy told him the strange wanderer had thrust the sword into the ash tree and had notified her and her astonished husband that only an appointed hero could pull the sword from the trunk.

She said many had attempted to extricate the weapon. All had failed.

Sigmond recalled how Wulf had promised him that one day, when he really needed a sword, he would find one in an unexpected place.

Well, he certainly needed one then.

And there was a sword in an unexpected place.

"I feel that the sword is yours to retrieve," the girl told her boyfriend.

"Go get it, and take me away from here. I hate Hagbard. I love you. Let's do it!"

"You will come with me, then?" Sigmond asked.

"I would go with you anywhere," Signy swore. "We were meant for each other."

"I think your husband felt that," Sigmond told her. "When he admitted that he abducted you, it was clear he reasoned that you were the sister I had mentioned as having been taken away when she was five.

"My sister's name was Signy," he told her.

"It comes back to me now," the lassie recalled. "My brother, my twin brother, was called Sigmond."

They kissed in mutual recognition.

Sigmond arose, went to the ash, seized the hilt of the sword and with a mighty flourish extracted it from the trunk.

Hastily dressed, and arm in arm, the couple fled out the door and into the forest, with the hero brandishing his new sword.

The fated couple were on their way to meet a destiny they felt had been awaiting them since birth.

Their father, Woden, had indeed plotted that destiny.

Chapter Six.
A MORAL DILEMMA

When Hagbard awoke at dawn with a massive headache, and found that his wife was not in bed with him, he became suspicious.

Despite the grogginess that was an aftereffect of the sleeping potion, he stormed out of bed and burst into the livingroom.

Just as he suspected. No wife. No guest. The door to the outside was left wide open.

And, although his vision was still somewhat blurred from his drugged sleep, he noticed that the sword was missing from the tree trunk.

Damn!

Hagbard did not stop for breakfast. He did not wash his face or comb his hair.

He knew the dastard had absconded with his wife.

But, they had not taken his horse.

Hagbard was a skilled woodsman and hunter. He could track a deer, a boar, or an enemy tribesman with precision.

With the motivation of revenge against an unfaithful wife and a home-wrecker, his highly honed abilities were heightened.

And being mounted in pursuit of the running fugitives, he felt assured of a very sweet revenge.

Sigmond led his sister/sweetheart towards the North Forest. Since he had been raised there, it was the region he knew best.

He realized that Hagbard would come looking for them in that area. But intimate knowledge of every tree, bush, cave, and mountain would be to the couple's advantage over their pursuer.

Looking down on the North Forest from the plateau atop Mount Utgard, Woden and his favorite daughter, the Valkyrie Brynhildr, were gazing down at the North Forest below.

The sheer precipice on the east side of the plateau made the location nearly inaccessible to most mortals.

Woden was aware that his twin children were in flight heading directly for Mount Utgard.

He had not revealed his master plan for retrieval of the ring and helmet to his Valkyrie daughters.

But he felt this was the right moment to tell Brynhildr that she had a half-brother and a half-sister heading their way. And that they were being pursued by an evil-doer who was intent on murdering them.

He did not go into detail about how the twins' unborn baby in Signy's womb was supposed to change the entire future of both gods and mortals.

As he was telling his daughter as much as he felt she needed to know, his raven, Munin landed on his shoulder and informed him that Hagbard was about to catch up with the fugitives on the meadow at the foot of the precipice.

Which, of course, meant that a battle to the death between Sigmond and Hagbard would take place any minute.

Woden needed Brynhildr to intervene in the battle. And, of course, in favor of her half-brother.

Brynhildr was delighted to discover that she had a heroic half-brother and a half-sister who was pregnant with the couple's baby.

Brynhildr, even though she claimed to be a virgin, had a moral compass more in alignment with her father's view than that of her step-mother, Frida.

Woden was delighted that his plan for getting back the ring was about to work out pretty much as he'd planned.

Brynhildr would see to it that Hagbard would be killed in the impending man-to-man battle.

Sigmond and Signy would settle down. Signy would bear the super-hero, Sigord.

The couple would raise the kid, who would inherit the super-sword his daddy had yanked out of the tree and would go dispatch Vanir, who had turned into a dragon.

Then, like a good little grandson should, Sigord would bring the ring to his loving grandpa. And Woden would not only still be king of the gods, but Master of the Age as well. He would be the possessor of infinite wealth and would have access to boundless nookie. At least, that was the plan. But...

As he was reveling in these happy thoughts, Munin flew down and landed on his shoulder.

"Psst!" Munin warned. "You'd better watch out, Boss. Here comes trouble."

"Meaning?" Woden asked.

"Your ever-loving wife is heading in this direction."

Brynhildr overheard the bird's warning and ran for cover behind a nearby boulder.

Woden scanned the distance with his eye, and, sure enough, as always, the raven spoke sooth.

It was Frida all right. And there was no question that she was in her super-bitchy vein. Royally.

"Well, good morning, Dear," Woden addressed his wife in as cheery a tone as he could muster.

"Don't you 'Good morning, Dear' me. You louse!" Frida replied.

"My sources tell me those twins you sired on that chippy Yrsa have found each other. And committed incest with each other. And if that weren't bad enough, the girl, Signy, is married. And what's more, she's knocked up with her brother's spawn in her belly.

"And if that's still not enough, you not only approve of this nasty little arrangement. It was all your stupid idea in the first place.

"And here I am. The goddess of wedlock, and the sanctity of marriage. I am at the forefront of the war against the sin of incest.

"We simply cannot have the gods championing the very foundation of civilization. Incest and adultery cannot be encouraged. And I will not allow you to condone this vile situation."

Woden could hardly get a word in edgewise.

But Frida stopped to take a breath and he leaped into the breach.

"Now, now, My Dear," he soothed. "You're all worked up. Look at this from the bright side.

"Your sister, Freya, is the goddess of love. What we have here is young love. Young love is beautiful…"

Frida cut in angrily.

"Cut the crap, Woden. You know as well as I do that, although my sister is the goddess of love, she does not condone immorality.

"What you are championing here isn't love. It is simply a matter of sibling teenagers making out. And committing adultery at the same time. To say nothing of incest.

"Those whelp of yours are in double moral jeopardy. I will not have it, Woden. Do you hear? I will not have us shaking the moral fabric of the entire world!"

At the moment, Woden could not see what Frida could do about it anyway. So he relaxed into letting her spew on.

But just as he was starting to relax, his wife changed course.

"My sources have also informed me, Husband, that your two incestuous kids are heading in this direction even as we speak."

"Uh-oh!"

And that Signy's husband is chasing after them. As is his right," she continued.

"I suppose you *do* agree that Hagbard, your son-in-law is within his rights to pursue his cheating wife."

She paused.

No response.

"Don't you, Woden?" Frida demanded.

What could Woden say? His wife was absolutely right. He had to respond.

"Yes, Dear."

"That crow of yours has probably informed you…" Frida went on.

"Raven!" the god interjected.

"That according to all sightings, the husband will catch up with his wife and the wife-snatcher right down there on that meadow you were gazing at."

No response from Woden.

"And, I'm just sure," Frida assured him, "that you plan to send one of your fat daughters down there to make sure that the husband, who is in the moral and legal right, loses the battle between him and that immoral son of yours."

Woden's pride was ruffled.

"My daughters are *not* fat!" he protested.

"I'm talking about the ones you begat through Yortha."

"The Valkyries," he assented. "They are *not* fat. They're big boned."

"Fat or big boned, I will not stand for you sending any of them down there to protect Sigmond. For the sake of the moral world we're supposed to be guarding, you cannot interfere to make the home-wrecker win."

Woden saw the point. And had to admit to himself that Frida was right.

But she did not see the big picture.

He explained to her, in detail, how he had to get the ring and the helmet back. And that he himself could not break the sacred contract and take them back from Vanir, who was their legal owner.

He had long ago worked out this clever plan, with Loki's help of course, to sire a hero son, who, in turn, would sire a super-hero son, who would be able to get the ring and helmet back without breaking any contract. So the ring would be in possession of the gods and not in the hands of some brutally stupid giant/dragon.

"You say the dragon is stupid!" Frida scoffed.

"I'd say the stupidity started with you."

She elaborated on her view.

Woden had gotten the silly idea that he needed a new castle, Valhalla.

He'd hired the dumbest creatures on earth, two giants, to build it for him. And as payment, he and Loki had offered Freya.

"That, in itself, beats all for a hare-brained idea. Where did you think you were going to get golden apples then? How did you plan to feed our mojo? And, offering the dumbasses your own dear sister-in-law as payment to boot. Dumb, dumb, dumb."

She then went on to tell how he had been outwitted by the slow-witted giant into letting go of the ring.

"And if that wasn't numb-skulled enough, you came up with the mad idea of getting that whore Yrsa pregnant with twins who were supposed to grow up, mate, and produce someone to go get the ring for you."

"Yrsa was not a whore," Woden protested.

He was right about that.

But deep down in his heart he knew that a god like himself, who had given up his left eye for a sip from the Norn's Well of Wisdom, had shown less than stellar qualities in his judgment.

As a final barb, Frida pointed out that the gold to craft ring and helmet had been stolen from Lord Wyrd. So it rightfully belonged to him, or to his daughters who had lost it to that Gnome thief Alvis.

She pointed out that not Vanir, not Alvis, and certainly not Woden had any legal claim to it.

"All right, all right, damn it," Woden capitulated.

"You're right. I admit it. I asked Brynhildr to go down to the meadow when the duel begins. I told her to intervene on behalf of Sigmond.

"Hagbard is a bad dude. No question. But, in this instance, I have to admit he's in the moral right.

"I'll order Brynhildr to see that Hagbard wins.

"Then I'll get together with Loki to figure out some other way to get hold of the damned ring and helmet."

"Promise on your spear, Husband," Frida demanded.

Reluctantly, the great god swore on his sacred spear.

His pledge was now irrevocable.

Thus, Woden had sworn that his beloved son would die.

He shed tears out of his good eye.

Chapter Seven.
BRYNHILDR'S FIREWALL

Frida was satisfied with herself. She had taken her stand on the solid side of righteousness.

She had put her husband in his place.

And so she returned to Valhalla with a smirk on her face.

When Frida had disappeared out of sight, Brynhildr came out from behind her boulder.

She had overheard the conversation between her father and her step-mother.

And was distressed that her father had wimped out.

When she returned to his side, Woden began to explain to her about the ring and helmet and about how both that little weasel of a Gnome and he himself both yearned to get it back from the dopy dragon who slept on top of it day and night, except when he came out of his cave for his drink. And to take a piss. Or snack on a mortal.

Brynhildr told him she knew all that now since she heard every word of the discussion with Frida.

"But, Daddy," she asked. "What do you really want me to do about the fight between Sigmond and Hagbard?"

"Didn't you hear me swear on my sacred spear that I would intervene to make Hagbard win?"

"I heard you say that," she answered. "But I cannot believe you really meant it that you want my half-bother to be killed by that no good scoundrel, Hagbard."

"Frida is right about the moral implications," Woden told her. "I still want you to go down there when Sigmond and Hagbard draw swords against each other. And I order you to make sure that Hagbard wins."

Brynhildr, be it noted, did not agree to do as her father had said.

As Woden left the scene so as not to have to observe his son get killed, Brynhildr muttered to herself, "I just cannot do that."

Brynhildr looked down from her height and saw Sigmond and Signy emerging from the forest into the meadow.

Signy ran joyfully out onto the open space.

Sigmond caught up with his sweetie and kissed her.

He picked her up, set her gently on the soft ground, and in a rapture made love to her for all he was worth.

The lovely sight filled Brynhildr with warm satisfaction.

Did she herself know the joy of sex?

No Anglo-Saxon bard ever knew the answer to that one.

But given what a randy crowd those Anglo-Saxon invaders of Britain are known to be, most contemporary scholars are doubtful about Brynhildr's virginity.

As Hagbard rode out of the forest he saw his previous guest fucking his wife in the open air, for anyone passing by to observe.

His wrath passed the limits of endurance.

As she spasmed in orgasm, Signy caught sight of her husband's approach and fainted.

Brynhildr figured it was high time to get down there where the action was soon to erupt.

Sigmond arose from his girlfriend's sweet side, drew his magic sword, and faced his approaching adversary.

Hagbard dismounted, sword in hand, and with rage in his eyes.

The battle of the wronged husband and the young lover began with a clash of steel.

Brynhildr, invisible to the combatants, protected Sigmond with her shield as Hagbard lunged towards him.

When Woden, who was slowly descending the mountain on the far, non-precipitous side of the plateau, heard the clash of steel on shield, he immediately sensed that his daughter was disobeying him.

He had to hie himself immediately to the battle scene to impose his will on the outcome.

When Brynhildr saw her father approach with his rage at being disobeyed evident in his glare, she retreated from the scene, found her horse Brida, rode to the spot where Signy lay unconscious on the meadow floor, swooped her up and rode to the forest edge.

Of course neither of the gladiators were aware of the divine drama that was playing out against their own life and death battle. Neither had any idea that the game was fixed.

Sigmond had gained a favorable position where with a lunge he could run his magic sword right into his opponent's heart.

At that moment, Woden struck his son's sword with his own sacred spear, shattering the sword into fragments.

Hagbard took advantage of the opportunity, and decapitated his mortal enemy with a single swipe.

Brynhildr laid her half-sister on the ground and rode hell bent for election to the site of the battle.

As she was thus engaged, Woden was busy running Hagbard through with his spear again and again in a violent rage in revenge for his son's death.

Brynhildr scooped up the fragments of Sigmond's sword, and while Woden was distracted by his wild fit of rage, she returned to Signy, laid her prostrate body back on her horse, and took off for the High Hills.

When Woden had expended his rage and despair on the man who had decapitated his son, he looked around.

He saw that both Signy and the remains of Sigmond's shattered sword had been taken away. Realizing what his daughter had done, he swore a great oath. An oath to punish his daughter Brynhildr for her disobedience.

In the High Hills there was a meeting place where the Valkyries regularly gathered.

Brynhildr brought Signy and the pieces of the magic sword to that gathering spot.

All eight of the other Valkyries were gathered there. They were acutely aware that a divine crisis was afoot.

They had been watching the battle in the meadow and the conflict between their father and their sister.

They observed Brynhildr spiriting away Signy and the shattered sword.

And Gondul, one of the sisters, was keeping a watch on their father.

Brynhildr arrived at the gathering spot. Signy had revived and was riding pillion on Brida. She was clasping the sword shards to her breast.

The buxom sisters hardly had time to greet their sibling and their half-sister when Gondul returned with a warning.

"Brynhildr. You've got to hide. Daddy will be here within the next five minutes."

"No, Girls," Brynhildr answered. "What we've got to do is get Signy away from here first. With the mood Daddy's in, she won't be safe.

"In her womb she's carrying the hero who can get Daddy and the rest of us out of the mess he's gotten us all into.

"We have to get Signy and her unborn baby away to somewhere that Daddy will not go to. And she has to take these pieces of Sigmond's broken sword and get it re-forged back into battle-ready condition.

"The only place in the world we know Daddy will not dare go to is to the part of the East Forest where Vanir sleeps in his cave guarding the ring, the helmet, and the rest of the crap Daddy handed over to him."

The sisters agreed.

So they set Signy back in Brida's saddle and made sure she had the sword shards safely in the saddle bag.

"Now don't forget," Brynhildr told Signy. "When you get to the East Forest, find a smith who can re-forge those scraps. The joker will be that only a man who knows no fear can accomplish the task.

"So go have your kid. Remember to name him Sigord. And find a smithy where a hero who knows no fear can re-forge the sword so Sigord can kill the dragon, get the ring, and bring it to Daddy. Oh, yeah. That helmet thingy, too. It's called a Tarn. And don't forget. The sword also has a name. It's Nodhung.

"It's the only way we can get our race of gods out of the screwed up mess our father has gotten us all into."

And with that good advice, Signy headed the horse eastward and was away from there just minutes before Woden arrived on the scene.

Woden arrived at the Valkyrie gathering spot.

And Boy! Was he ever pissed off!

"Where is that traitor daughter of mine?" he roared.

"Standing right here waiting for you, Daddy," Brynhildr said demurely.

Woden dismounted and faced his miscreant daughter eyeball to eyeballs.

"How dared you disobey me, you ungrateful child?" the king of the gods spat out.

"You know as well as I do, Daddy, that I did what you *really* wanted me to do," she answered. "Deep down in your heart you know that unless you can get hold of the ring, either a giant will use it to destroy us. Or a Gnome will get it back. And then all Hell will break loose.

"Who cares what Frida says about that marriage and incest crap? Our very existence is in jeopardy until you get the gods damned ring back.

"And besides, Sigmond was your son and our brother. And we all know Hagbard was such an asshole."

Woden had to chew all that over.

But he had his wife Frida to face. And that fact trumped everything else.

"Don't you dare challenge my judgment," he blustered.

"I gave you orders. No matter what crazy idea you get in your mind, you Valkyries *must* obey orders.

"So, Brynhildr. Prepare to hear your sentence."

"Yes, Daddy," agreed his truly dutiful daughter.

She knew she had obeyed her father's innermost wish.

But she was prepared to take her punishment without further protest like the true warrior she was.

"Since you failed to discharge your duty of absolute obedience, which is required of a Valkyrie, I demote you from the race of the gods and make you a mortal," the king of the gods decreed.

Brynhildr felt in her flesh and bones the painful transformation from immortality to mortality.

She had never really considered the meaning of death before.

She hadn't been able to conceive that there could be any ending to her being.

Now she was aware that there was a limit to her very existence.

It was the opposite of what happened to the fallen heroes she had gathered from the world's battlefields. They metamorphosed from mortals to immortal guards of Valhalla.

This change of status was instantaneous and caused her sisters to weep on her behalf.

The idea of losing a sister to death had heretofore simply been unthinkable.

Brynhildr could see from Woden's expression that he had not yet declared the remainder of the sentence.

She awaited the rest of his verdict standing dutifully at attention.

"What is more," Woden continued. "You will lose your cherry to the first mortal who encounters you. And you will be subject to him for so long as you both shall live, as though wedded."

The virginity question, as we have noted, is a moot point among modern epicologists.

There is no evidence among the Anglo-Saxon epics that Brynhildr responded to her father on that point of his sentence.

But being ravaged sexually and joined for the rest of her life to any fool, coward, or bounder who came around next! That was simply too much.

For the first time in her life Brynhildr broke down in tears.

Her sisters' sobs joined hers and echoed throughout the High Hills.

Woden was moved.

He truly loved Brynhildr. Of all his many, many offspring, the result of ages of philandering, Brynhildr was by far his favorite.

As he considered the sentence he had imposed in anger, he searched his mind for a mitigating factor.

He put the entire matter on hold until he could summon Loki to help him resolve the issue without reversing a word of what he had already declared.

Woden sent Munin out to find Loki and summon him to the spot.

There never was a raven more responsive than Munin. He rapidly found Loki, who was up to some unspecified mischief that is probably best left untold anyway.

And when he was told of Brynhildr's sentence, Loki was on the spot with Woden, Brynhildr, and the fat sisters in a trice.

He was by far the fastest moving of the gods. And he was quite fond of Brynhildr.

She had more of a sense of humor than any of the stodgy dwellers of Valhalla. And she had less respect for Frida's middle-class morality than any of the gods. Including Woden.

She was Loki's kind of goddess.

When he arrived at Woden's side, Loki agreed that there was no part of the sentence that could be reversed.

"But," he reasoned. "there is no reason to subject Brynhildr to the lust of any bloke who comes along her way.

"What we have to do, here, Woden, is put her to sleep in this remote corner of the High Hills.

"You won't find your average bozo wandering into this rugged area.

"And I can set up a firewall around her. I'm talking about a raging inferno of a firewall. No one but a fearless hero would even consider barging through it for the sake of a little hanky-panky with our girl here."

Brynhildr picked up at the idea.

She had accepted the idea of becoming a mortal. And she had no objection to being fucked and virtually married to a mortal.

Providing that mortal was as strong, as fearless, and as heroic as she herself was.

The firewall would protect her from dweebs, wimpeys, drunks, and bozos.

"All right, then," she declared to her father. "Bring it on."

Woden bade Brynhildr lie down on the soft, grassy earth that covered Mount Utgard, the highest of the High Hills.

He put her to sleep.

She would not awake from that sleep until kissed by the man who was fearless enough to break through the turbulent ring of fire that would surround her and kiss her.

Brynhildr fell into her deep coma.

Loki, the god of fire, set up the awesome, intimidating circle of flames around her.

Woden, Loki, and the Valkyries had nothing more to do at the site. They got on their steeds and returned to Valhalla.

Meanwhile, Signy continued on to the East Forest to play her role in the drama she was destined to engage in to redeem both gods and men.

Chapter Eight.
SIGORD FORGES A SWORD

Brynhildr's horse bore Signy eastward until it brought her to the location shunned by Woden. Namely to the clearing near the cave in which Vanir slept atop his treasure, which included the ring and the helmet.

We need to remember that, through the agency of the Tarn helmet, Vanir had shifted his shape to that of a monstrous, vicious man-eating dragon.

In that shape he was content to sleep through most of the day and night. At high noon he roused himself, emerged from his cave, looked around to see if there was anyone close by he could eat, and then he pressed forward just far enough to get to the freshwater pool that lay in the shadow of the edge of the forest.

After enjoying a nice cool drink and a pleasant piss he dragged himself back into the shelter of his cave and dozed off until noon the following day.

In the clearing, the two Gnome brothers, Alvis and Mim, had constructed huts where they could keep watch over the sleeping dragon.

Alvis had a vested interest in retrieving the ring. He felt he had paid for it with his balls and thus deserved it back.

Although Alvis had actually forged the ring, Mim had coached him on some technical points. And he was the one who had created the helmet. And he felt quite sure he deserved both ring and helmet more than his less gifted, ball-less brother.

Each one spent many hours of the day attempting to develop a plan to get the two wondrous artifacts, plus the valuable hoard of treasure, away from the awesome dragon.

To keep himself busy, Mim set up a forge in the open in front of his hut, where he worked with such metal as he could accumulate.

Alvis, the less skillful of the brothers, did not set up a forge. He chose to devote every waking moment keeping watch over the dragon's cave, hoping an opportunity of any kind would present itself to distract the monster.

When Brida brought Signy to the clearing, both brothers were very aware of her arrival.

Alvis did not see how the girl could benefit him. Perhaps if he still had his balls it would be another matter altogether. But, considering his condition, he chose to ignore her.

Mim thought the young lady might just deliver. And, if not, he might perhaps find a way to use her to lure Vanir out of his cave and into the forest, leaving time for a fleet-footed Gnome to get in and out of the cave before the monster's return.

As it turned out, Signy was a disappointment in the loving department. In the first place, she was pregnant. In the second place she found Mim disgusting. (Who didn't?) And in the third place she was true to her deceased hero boyfriend.

In due time, Signy gave birth to her son, Sigord, in Mim's hut.

She died in childbirth.

But before she died, she handed Mim the shards from Sigmond's sword.

As she lay dying, she thanked her Gnome benefactor.

"Thank you, Mim, for giving me shelter and for caring for me during my pregnancy. Take care of my newborn son. I name him Sigord.

"Raise him to be a credit to you, his foster-father, and to Sigmond, his biological father.

"I entrust these broken bits of Sigmond's sword to you. They can once again be forged into a magic sword for my son to use against the forces of evil.

"The shards can only be forged into a mighty weapon called Nodhung by one who knows no fear.

"That may be you. I do not know. Or it may be another smith within your world. Again, I do not know."

And with those words, Signy died.

Mim was delighted to be rid of the bitch.

And he figured the re-forged sword could be used to slay the dragon and retrieve the treasure.

His plan was to raise this kid, Sigord. Forge that magic sword, Nodhung And when the boy got old enough, send him into the cave to kill the dragon.

With any luck, Sigord would slay the dragon and the dragon would kill Sigord.

Then all Mim would have to do was get the ring and the helmet out from under the monster and he would be the shape-shifting, visible/invisible Master of the Age.

He could hardly wait for the brat to grow up.

By the time he was eight years old, Sigord left the hut right after breakfast every morning with the swords and spears Mim made for him.

He always returned home by lunchtime with meat for Mim to cook.

He not only killed the animals he hunted, he skinned and butchered them as well.

Mim and Sigord ate much better than their neighbor Alvis who, alas was not much of a hunter. Nor, for that matter, much of a cook either.

While his foster-son was out getting meat for the table, Mim worked tirelessly with the scraps of the magical sword.

He tried very hard to learn to be fearless so that he could accomplish the job.

But, alas, he was a congenital scardy-cat.

As Sigord grew stronger and stronger with age, he kept breaking the swords and spears Mim forged for him.

Mim had told him about his father's fabulous sword. Sigord urged Mim to keep trying harder to make it into a sword for him. He was confronting ever larger, fiercer, and more dangerous animals in the forest and needed more robust blades and spear points.

Of course Sigord knew about the dragon that slept in the cave across the clearing. It was pretty hard to ignore. He certainly would like a chance to confront it as he fearlessly met every other creature in the East Forest.

And Mim constantly encouraged him in this goal. It was, after all, the whole purpose he had in mind from the time the little bugger was born. The kid wielding the sword was, as we know, Mim's master plan for grabbing the ring, the helmet, and the hoard, and lording it over everyone in the world – including his detestable brother who didn't seem to be good for anything except keeping his toenails clipped.

One day, when he was sixteen years old, Sigord returned from his hunt empty-handed.

He had encountered a bear. His spear broke against the bear's hide, really pissing the bear off something fierce.

Sigord then ran the bear through its slathering maw with his sword. But the sword went down the beast's throat, without killing it.

Sigord then wrestled the bear, got a chokehold on it and strangled it.

He retrieved the sword, only to find that it wasn't sharp enough to skin the bear, much less butcher it.

He returned to the hut in a foul, foul temper.

"Gods damn it to Hel (the Anglo-Saxon Hell)," he stormed at his foster-father.

"This sword business just really gets my balls in an uproar. You're supposed to be such a hotshot smith. And all I get for weapons from you is shit.

"Get me those fucking scraps of metal my mom gave you from my real daddy's sword."

Mim bustled over to the spot where he kept the valuable stash and brought it, wordlessly, to Sigord.

"If *you* can't get the job done, let's see what *I* can do," the lad demanded.

Mim was quite sure the boy, without even having apprentice training, could not manage to do anything more than make a mess.

But why not humor the big bastard? What was there to lose?

Sigord had observed Mim at his forge and anvil all his life. Smithing was Gnome's work, and Sigord had always felt, as the son of a hero, that it was beneath him.

But he needed a decent sword. And the cocksucking Gnome wasn't getting the job done.

So he was willing, on this one occasion, to stoop to the level of a smith.

Mim fired up the forge.

Sigord inserted the crucible containing the magic metal into the forge.

He hammered the metal into shape on the anvil.

He plunged the work into the water.

He demanded that Mim bring him a hilt.

And, because Sigord truly was absolutely fearless, he was successful in forging the weapon that was the sword of destiny, Nodhung.

Mim wondered why he hadn't thought of getting the damned kid to do the job before. He knew that the son of a bitch was arrogant. He just somehow hadn't before connected the word arrogant with the word fearless.

"Come on, Asshole" Sigord now commanded his foster-father.

"It will soon be noon. Let's get our asses over to the mouth of the dragon's cave. When he comes out for his noontime drink and piss, I want to be ready to meet that foul monster."

Just what Mim had been waiting for for sixteen years.

"Just a moment," Mim pleaded. "I have something I need to do first."

He was speaking to the empty air. Sigord was already on his way, brandishing his wondrous sword in heroic flourishes.

Mim had been saving a flask of deadly poison for just this occasion.

He was confident Sigord would slay the dragon.

If, in the event, the dragon did not kill the tiresome kid, Mim needed a horn of poison to offer Sigord after the battle. He had one ready.

Horn of poison in hand, Mim shagged his fat arse out the door and across the clearing. He sat at the edge of the forest where he could watch the drama unfold that he had waited for for years.

As Sigord stood between the mouth of the cave and the forest edge he asked Mim, "Do you think a dragon's heart is in the same location as the other creatures I've killed and butchered?"

Mim told him that was probably the case. But also admitted that he knew precious little about the anatomy of dragons.

Sigord was satisfied that he would know where to jab at the monster

when the opportunity presented itself. He reasoned that the beast would need to rise up facing him at some point in the coming battle.

Sigord now had his battle strategy.

Alvis was sitting on his door stoop fascinated at what he was observing.

Mim's brat was posturing in the clearing, waving a sword at the entrance to Vanir's cave.

The big lunk apparently was stupid enough to want to fight the monster.

Great!

While they were fighting, he might be able to sneak into the cave and retrieve the ring he'd given up his balls for.

Cool!

At precisely high noon, everyone outside the cave could hear Vanir yawn and stretch.

The stretch worked out the monster's kinks and a sleepy-eyed, groggy dragon head emerged from the cave.

It looked around to see if there might be anyone eatable in the immediate neighborhood.

Oh, ho!

The dragon's head was no longer of somnolent cast. The eyes fairly sparkled with delight.

A delightful mouthful of human meat was standing before him, waving some kind of metal stick. Perhaps a sword.

With a lunge Vanir emerged from his cave shooting venom from his fangs.

Nuts! Missed!

The human male laughed.

Worse, he scoffed.

That simply would not do.

Vanir raised a leg, aimed his pecker at the loathsome human, and tried to piss venom on Sigord.

The action made his tail vulnerable.

Sigord dodged the venomous piss, scooted aside, and cut the end of the tail off the dragon.

The worthy sword had proved itself.

Vanir reared up in pain and anger, emitting a fearful roar.

In doing so, he exposed his breast.

Sigord knew the vulnerable spot. With a mighty lunge, he drove his sword – his father's trusty sword – directly into the heart of the beast.

Vanir, the dragon, fell, dead, with a thunk, onto the ground.

As Sigord withdrew his sword, drops of blood from the expiring dragon spotted his right hand.

Sigord sucked the blood off his fingers.

Sigord was not aware of something you, we, and countless many others know. Namely, that if you drink even a very small amount of dragon blood, you can understand what the birds and beasts say to you.

No sooner had Sigord ingested the dragon blood than he heard a bird in a nearby tree tell him, "Quick, Boy. Get into the cave. There is a ring and a helmet in there, resting on a pile of treasure. Scoot in there, grab those trinkets and get out before the Gnomes get in."

Alvis and Mim did not understand bird talk so were not aware of what the damned bird was twittering about.

They didn't feel they needed to. They'd been waiting for a break like this for years.

When the dwarves saw the dragon die, they ran towards the cave entrance. They had to circle Vanir's grotesque corpse from opposite sides, and collided with each other.

The impact knocked them both out.

As Sigord exited the cave with his two treasures he skirted around the unconscious Gnomes, avoided the dragon's corpse, and went to stand beneath the tree where the helpful bird was perching.

The bird told him not to trust either of the Gnomes. So Sigord was wary when Mim recovered consciousness and approached him with a drinking horn.

"Well done, Lad," Mim congratulated. "I have brought you a victory horn to slake the thirst of post-battle."

Sigord received the horn.

The bird told him, "Beware, Hero. The drink is poisoned. Kill the two Gnomes."

Alvis recovered from his swoon and noticed at once that the stupid kid was wearing the gods damned ring.

And that he was pouring some liquid from a horn down Mim's throat.

He saw that Mim went directly into paroxysms.

Good! That was the end of the tiresome brother.

But Alvis knew this was not a good time to hang around to see whether the teenager was in a generous or a cranky mood.

Before his brother had made his last death gurgle, Alvis was out of there and heading for Gnomeland as rapidly as little legs would carry him.

Leaving the body of his treacherous foster-father on the ground where he lay, Sigord dragged the giant dragon's body to the cave entrance. He arranged it to block access to the treasure that remained within.

That task finished, he returned to the base of the tree to sprawl out in the shade and converse with his new-found little feathered friend.

You might ask what finally happened to ball-less little Alvis.

No one ever seemed to know or care.

Chapter Nine.
SIGORD GETS A GIRLFRIEND

The bird told Sigord that he had been entrusted with directions to lead him to the woman Destiny (Wyrd) had waiting for him.

Sigord told the bird he had no idea what the word *Wyrd* even meant.

"Few creatures have any real concept of destiny (fate)," the bird replied. "I do not. Nor does it matter. The only thing I have ever heard about it is that Lord Wyrd knows what it is, and he directs it."

All that was way too much for the hero to ponder. Or even to care about.

Something he *did* care about was that there apparently was a babe out there who was available.

Available ladies had interested the lad very much now for a few years.

When hunting in the East Forest, he did, of course, track game. But there was also loving aplenty in the woods for a husky, good-looking young stud to track.

If the bird was ready to lead him to some of that, he felt he could use some about now.

The bird even told him the name of his new sweetie.

It was Brynhildr.

Sigord asked what she looked like.

Apparently that was not knowledge to which the bird was privy.

Nor, when Sigord inquired about sweet love-making did the fine-feathered guide show any comprehension of what the kid was talking about.

Bird and lad progressed in a generally westerly direction. They paused from time to time to discuss the time of day, the weather, and other prosaic matters with hares, bears, snakes, toads, and other creatures.

There was an understood truce between hunter and edible creatures during the journey. So conversations were all civil.

171

When bird and hero got to the foot of the High Hills, the bird bade the lad farewell.

"Continue in the direction you are now heading," said the flying guide. "You will see roaring flames atop one of the hills. That will not be a forest fire.

"If you have the balls to walk through the raging flames, you will encounter Brynhildr.

"If you shy away from the possibility of being fricasseed, you know your way back to Mim's hut and to the treasure in the near-by cave.

"Farewell."

And on that note the hero was left to face the task ahead. Or reject it.

In Sigord's case, this was a no-brainer. Since he knew no fear, breaking through a wall of flames was not any kind of problem whatsoever.

He pressed on and at length spied the fire atop Mount Utgard.

Knowing what was enclosed within that fire made the hero horny. He hastened up the mountain, took a deep breath and plunged through the flames with his sword held high, yearning for nookie.

When he arrived within the enclosed space, there she was as promised.

Sigord had never encountered a girl or woman he did not like. Some were better than others. Of course. But sex was all good.

Yet, to his taste, the number one prime lover-girl of all was fat (large-boned, saftig, juicy) and mature (older, experienced, grateful).

Brynhildr was everything Sigord could ever want in a woman.

But, since she was in a very deep sleep, it seemed to him a good time to check out the merchandise.

Brynhildr turned out to be easy to undress.

Sure, she was hefty. But he was strong. She was armored but he tore the metal off in a trice.

And her robe beneath the cuirass was not at all difficult to slip off.

Sigord had already gotten a good gander at her face.

A moon-faced beaut!

As soon as he got a good look at those giant tits he was ready for love.

Wunderbar!

He satisfied his foot fetish before flipping her over to explore her lovely, ample arse.

He flipped her back over, face up.

It took no little birdie to tell him to kiss those full, sensual lips. And he somehow knew that would awaken her. And he needed her awake.

Sigord was not one to make love to an unresponsive broad. He craved enthusiastic action on the part of his partner.

Brynhildr awoke to find a young naked husky stud lying atop her with his tongue in her mouth and a hardon against her naked skin.

She was not a bit drowsy after her long nap.

She was ready for action.

So, without the benefit of foreplay, the two made up for lost time.

There was post-play aplenty, and a resumption of coitus to follow.

But there was very little in the way of conversation over the next few hours.

When they did get around to pillow talk, Brynhildr asked her swain who he was.

From his answers she determined that he was her nephew, Sigord.

She explained to him what an aunt was and instructed him never, ever, to call her Aunt Brynhildr.

Which he never did.

Munin was flying over the romantic scene the whole time.

He flew back to Valhalla and told Woden that his daughter and his grandson were whooping it up in the High Hills. That he'd spotted the ring on Sigord's finger and the Tarn helmet on the ground.

His raven's sense told him Brynhildr was already knocked up, and was already gestating Woden's simultaneous grandson and great grandson in her womb.

Woden was delighted. His and Loki's wonderful plan had worked out after all. The ring and helmet were practically his.

He called Loki, who turned off the fire that had surrounded the hot couple.

Woden sent one of his Valkyries down to the Mount Utgard to bring his two love-struck kids up to Valhalla so he could hug them (and get the gods damned ring).

(It was a big exception to the rules to have any mortals visit Valhalla. But that was hardly the only rule Woden had ever broken.)

The kids were happy.

Frida wasn't all that pleased with the consanguinity problem. But said she could live with it if the kids got married.

No problem.

Loki, of all gods, officiated at the ceremony.

Sigord gave the ring and helmet to his father-in-law/grandfather without a murmur.

And Goldul, one of the Valkyries, whisked the happy couple back down to earth, to the East Forest, where the vast treasure awaited them in Vanir's cave.

Chapter Ten.
TWILIGHT OF THE GODS

Woden felt he should be happy and content.

The great struggle for the ring was over, and he was the victor.

The ring adorned his finger, so he was Master of the Age.

It seemed an empty victory.

What did it really mean to be Master of the Age?

Of what worth was that enormous power?

He recalled the curse that Alvis had hurled at the ring when it was wrenched from him.

The malediction was that the ring would do no more good for its future owners than it had done for him.

When Woden considered the history of the owners of the ring since it had left Alvis' finger, he realized that the curse had held true.

Now that it adorned his own hand, he suspected that the curse still clung to it.

He needed to go wherever, or visit whomever, he could to get an answer to the questions that tormented him regarding the treasured jewelry that he had finally acquired.

He trusted the ring to respond to that desire.

And even as he mouthed the wish, he found himself transported to the root of Yggdrasil, the Universe Ash Tree.

And there, seated on a stately throne, sat the Lord of Wyrd.

"You need not ask me the questions you seek the answers to, Woden, King of the Gods and Master of the Age. I can read them in your heart," the great lord told him.

"I will add to the wisdom you acquired when you traded your eye to my daughters, the Norns, in exchange for a sip from the Well of Wisdom.

"And I will not exact payment from you of any bodily part for the wisdom I will now impart to you.

"I will tell you what you need to know and leave it up to you whether you feel a need to pay for the information or not.

"Know, Woden, that there are nine ages in the history of our Universe."

The lord waited for Woden's response.

"Are there more universes than ours, then, Lord Wyrd?" Woden asked.

The majestic lord chuckled.

"There are more universes than even I can count or imagine," the wise Lord replied.

"Our universe, the only one we are allowed to know about, is supported by Yggdrasil, the ash tree which you are privileged to observe at this moment.

"There are nine ages that grow on the tree, all connected to each other in one way or another.

"Your age, the Age of the Gods, Asgard, is the sixth in the sequence.

"It must conclude at some point to give way to the Age of Humankind, Mithgard.

"That age will be ruled by mortals, human beings, like your descendents from the union of Sigord and Brynhildr."

Woden suddenly understood that his action in making his beloved daughter mortal, and by his mortal grandson's union with her, his own descendents could be a part of the age to come.

The Lord of Wyrd continued.

"The ages that succeed Mithgard may not be revealed to you, Woden. And you have no need to know anything about them.

"But I can tell you that your age, Asgard, will end by fire. Valhalla and the gods of the current age will be consumed in flames."

Woden felt a need to inquire when that would occur.

"The end of this age and the beginning of the next one will transpire," the lord intoned, "When the debt owed to me is paid."

Woden was very aware of the weight of the ring on his finger.

He knew that the ring, which brings no happiness to its owner, The Master of the Age, must eventually be returned to its true owner in order to bring on the end of one age and the beginning of the next.

And he was fully aware of who the true owner was.

In all the sagas of the Gods of Northwest Europe that come down to us from the Sixth Century, that is where the story ends.

In the Seventh Century, Augustine of Canterbury brought Christianity to England.

The new religion pronounced anathema on the gods the Anglo-Saxons had brought with them to the Island.

In all the nations that worshipped Woden, Wotan, Odin, or any of the other names borne by the king of the gods, the same conflict between the new religion and the old one was waged.

Those who believed that Woden still wore the ring and mastered their age were of one faith. Those who believed Woden had returned the ring to the Sea of Wyrd, bringing on the Age of Mithgard were of a contrary faith.

The Venerable Bede told his readers that the old Anglo-Saxon tales had been superseded by Christianity, and to take the tales about Valhalla as nothing but fiction.

The individual choice of what to believe remains a matter for each of us to personally make.

About the Author
TIM DESMONDES

Tim Desmondes and his wife reside in Southern California.

Tim is the author of nine books other than the present volume published by the Nazca Plains Publishing Company:

- Sex and Loathing in Hollywood
- Sexual Diversity and Perversity in California
- Dracula Sucks Hollywood Dudes
- Venus Does Adonis While Apollo Shags a Tree
- Arthur Does Camelot
- Whores, Love and Pistols in the Wild West
- Robin's Too Tight Tights
- Sex and Love in Paris and Frisco
- Agnes Sorel: The Breast and Crotch that Changed History

If you enjoyed Beowulf, Wulfgar and their Friggin' Horny Gods you might want to enter Tim's world where you will meet other characters who have shared their stories with Tim, who, in turn will share their stories with you.

Desmondes

Arthur Does Camelot

Arthur
Does Camelot

a novel by
Tim Desmondes

Desmondes

Dracula Sucks
Hollywood Dudes

Dracula Sucks Hollywood Dudes

Tim Desmondes

Desmondes

Inside Robin's Too Tight Tights

inside
ROBIN'S
too tight tights

a novel by
Tim Desmondes

Desmondes

Sex and Loathing in
HOLLYWOOD

SEX AND LOATHING IN HOLLYWOOD

Tim Desmondes

Desmondes

Whores, Love and Pistols
In the Wild West

WHORES, LOVE AND PISTOLS

a novel by
Tim Desmondes

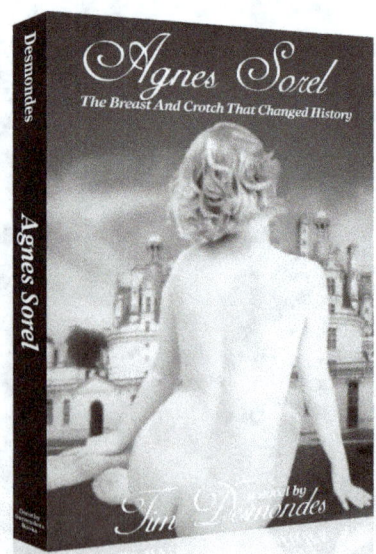

Desmondes

Agnes Sorel
The Breast And Crotch That Changed History

Agnes Sorel

a novel by
Tim Desmondes

www.ingramcontent.com/pod-product-compliance
Lightning Source LLC
Chambersburg PA
CBHW071209260626
47162CB00004B/1226